THE
PHOTOGRAPHER
IN SEARCH OF
DEATH

THE PHOTOGRAPHER IN SEARCH OF DEATH

STORIES OF THE REAL AND THE MAGICAL

MICHAEL MIROLLA

Publishers of Singular
Fiction, Poetry, Nonfiction, Translation, Drama and Graphic Books

Library and Archives Canada Cataloguing in Publication

Mirolla, Michael, 1948-, author
The photographer in search of death : stories of the real and magical
/ Michael Mirolla.

Issued in print and electronic formats.
ISBN 978-1-55096-686-2 (softcover).--ISBN 978-1-55096-687-9 (EPUB).--
ISBN 978-1-55096-689-3 (Kindle).--ISBN 978-1-55096-690-9 (PDF)

I. Title.

PS8576.I76P46 2017   C813'.54   C2017-905879-7
                                          C2017-905880-0

Published by Exile Editions ~ www.ExileEditions.com
Printed and Bound in Canada by Marquis.

We gratefully acknowledge the Canada Council for the Arts,
the Government of Canada, the Ontario Arts Council,
and the Ontario Media Development Corporation
for their support toward our publishing activities.

Canadian sales representation:
The Canadian Manda Group, 664 Annette Street,
Toronto ON M6S 2C8   www.mandagroup.com   416 516 0911

North American and international distribution, and U.S. sales:
Independent Publishers Group, 814 North Franklin Street,
Chicago IL 60610   www.ipgbook.com   toll free: 1 800 888 4741

To family, naturally,
but especially the newest generation:
Gabriel, Christopher, Daniel, Briallen.

THE POSSESSION

As always, Amil pops out of the trunk first, rotating his head in a 360-degree circle to examine his surroundings: an empty nondescript room whose lack of windows gives the impression of a disguised bunker.

All clear, he says, looking back into the trunk.

Wolf emerges, blinking, eyes rimmed red.

I hope you're right this time, he says, dabbing at his eyes with a handkerchief. No more surprises.

The two men – somewhat past, as the saying goes, their prime – have always shared the same room. Not the same room in the sense of one room but rather a series of identical rooms accumulated over a period of many years. But it might as well have been one room for all it matters: bedroom-living room-bathroom-kitchen nook all crammed in one space. And, while they are free to leave the room and wander about, they always return before nightfall, as if tethered by some type of umbilical cord.

Contrary to malicious gossip, however, it isn't because of some mutual attraction, a lust for one another that makes everything else – even the possibility of disease and excruciating death – irrelevant. Nor are they related – at least not by blood. No, the truth, as is usually the case, seems of the much more mundane variety. You see, they own something in common which neither is willing to relinquish completely to the other. This…shall we say…possession had been acquired just prior to the sharing of that first, primal room, now so indistinguishable from the rest. And both have a vague memory of having come from different elsewheres, of journeys of some kind, a memory that seems to manifest itself in languages neither of them understand – at least not on a conscious level. What they do know is that, unless they are really forced to, they do not want to experience such vagueness or journeys ever again.

After all those decades together, filled with the cares and necessities of daily life, the unstudied routines of existence, neither any longer can actually come out and say what this possession might be – or why it is so important. Is it perhaps the antique, stretched-to-the-limit almost transparent table-lamp cover that popped up just after the last great war, after the annihilation of so much historic property? Amil says no. Wolf says yes. Or is it the massive black trunk – Prop. of A.H. & B.M. written on its side – they use when shifting from identical room to identical room? Wolf says no. Amil says yes. How about the cloudy-glassed bottles with labels that read: "*Olio di ricino – Manganello*"? Both shrug. The solution is obvious – to hold on to all their possessions jointly until the unique object is re-discovered. This presupposes, however, that they also have to hold on to each other, and never be out of one another's sight – at least while in the room. It is, as one might guess, this aspect of the arrangement that caused – and continues to cause – problems.

Wolf, a self-described "painter, architect, author, sensitive soul full of romantic aspirations that had been dashed before fruition," at first found this intolerable. He had fretted about his lack of privacy and his inability to act out his dreams with someone else in the room. In fact, he'd packed up to leave several times in those crazy early days when the relationship had yet to stabilize. Gradually, he has given up any thoughts of leaving. A voracious reader, spending much of his free time in the closest library he can find, Wolf claims to know about such things as symbols and metaphors and semiotics, and thus inevitably develops a theory concerning the possession.

2

It is non-existent, I tell you, he says, pacing as he imagined Socrates might have done. Simply a ruse invented by you to keep us together, to keep our détente going. After all, what would you do without me? You would have nothing to clean up, nothing to worry your little brain about. There's no doubt who the leader is around here. And you have intentions on my body. Oh, I know. You've held them in check till now but they'll surface one of these days. They'll burst forth. You mark my words. That bulge in your pants says more about you than all your excuses and wimpy apologies put together. That bulge defines you. That and your hairy chest. Like all your kind, you allow the physical to dictate how you conduct yourself. I, on the other hand, allow culture to dictate mine.

He also knows some of the theories behind sadomasochistic relationships (having read *The Legacy of Cain, The 120 Days of Sodom, Kannibale von Rotenburg, The Serpent in Paradise, Justine ou les Malheurs de la vertu, Histoire de Juliette, ou les Prospérités du vice*). Except, that in this particular case he can't decide which is which or who is who. Let alone what is what.

Every Monday, whether the urge is there or not, they strip down and fight. Evenly matched physically (Wolf short and wiry; Amil short and stocky), these bouts are usually decided by an opponent's slip, a new feint, an inventive grapple. As well, they are able to wrestle without causing too much damage to each other (except the one time when, in the heat of the moment, Amil had bitten Wolf on the buttock – and to prevent a reccurrence Amil is now obliged to remove his teeth before combat). During these wrestling matches, the two engage in a ritual litany of insults. But, although the tone seems to mark them as insults, neither really understands the specifics nor how they relate to them. An example:

Wolf: May you hang upside down until your testicles fall off.

Amil: May you spend your last days in a burning hut.

In keeping with the idea that only the joint possession holds them together, they won't acknowledge each other if they happen to meet on the street. Not even a nod or second look. They are strangers till they return to the room where, each night according to a pre-arranged schedule, first one and then the other examines and catalogues every article they own. It is probably true that most of these articles hadn't been found or bought together; nevertheless, they are now possessed jointly. Both allow this to happen – as long as the objects remain. A pair of reading spectacles ("Ruhnke Opticians") will one day be uncovered by Amil, on the next used by Wolf; pants and coats ("Lattimer Collection") are shared; a black fez with eagle decoration is worn by each on alternate days.

Amil rejects Wolf's theory. In fact, rejects all theories. Despite vague recollections of having been a teacher, or perhaps some type of civic leader or union organizer, he prides himself in being a practical man, a man of the world. He insists the possession is real – and somewhere to be found. The problem is that they haven't searched well enough. And he feels it is quite possible it will turn up at any moment, fresh and unharmed by the passage of all these years. This is possible even if nothing has appeared in the previous search. Amil's views are bolstered by the fact new things do materialize each time they examine their possessions, thus necessitating an updated catalogue daily. Not that *the* possession has turned up as yet, but it is only a matter of time before it does appear – or re-appear, to be more precise. Precision is Amil's outstanding attribute. When asked, he tells the time precisely, down to the second; measurements are precise; thoughts are precise; the world is a precise place with one word for every object or action – and should be run like a train schedule. It was his idea, for example, to examine their room nightly. Wolf hadn't been in favour at first, saying he knew its contents by heart. But he quickly changed his mind when he saw that Amil was going ahead without him and finding things never before seen.

The balance in the room – between living space, kitchen nook and the accumulation of material goods – is kept by the judicious disappearance of articles at crucial moments when the piles of clothes, furniture, baubles and antiques threatens to inundate them. There are no set rules for these disappearances, neither priority nor value of goods. Newly found as well as ancient articles vanish; important and trivial alike. Like all men who consider themselves important, Amil and Wolf have developed a very *laissez faire* attitude towards these articles and they are quickly forgotten in their all-consuming search for *the* possession. This possession is conceived in terms of everlastingness or indestructibility. It has simply been misplaced for the moment and both look forward with great anticipation to the day it will make itself found.

To date, their discoveries appear to have been of a random nature, without any discernible pattern that they can make out. But, of late, the objects they turn up are becoming increasingly nefarious. In rapid succession, a shotgun (with "A.H." beneath the trigger guard), a gold-plated pistol, a silver knife and a cudgel (inscribed with "Dux") are unearthed. Wolf attributes this to Amil's evil thoughts. He's decided long before that the articles appear and disappear through the action of their minds, a fused telekinesis, a link also buried in the past. That he's never been able to consciously think up an article doesn't deter him from formulating what he calls his "thought-article-thought" theory.

Amil doesn't help. He greets the theory with laughter and denies all connection between the articles and his thoughts even when pinned to the ground by Wolf one Monday and forced to say "thought-article-thought" several times in succession. These moments of sweaty intimacy can normally be put to good use by Wolf when he comes out on top. For one thing, he is able to extract confessions which otherwise wouldn't be forthcoming. Amil enjoys confessing – that he fantasizes winning an argument on genetic purity with Pope Pius XII; that he once voted for a socialist party; that he masturbates while imagining a steam engine chugging along and pulling into a station. But, of the strange and potentially hazardous articles of late, he admits to knowing nothing, even when Wolf comes dangerously close to snapping his forearm. Accompanying the appearance of these weapons is the vanishing of useful and time-worn articles such as their beds, shoes and underwear, things which have never disappeared before.

Amil laughs it all away. Sticking the gun, knife and cudgel in his pants and shouldering the shotgun, he goes off singing songs in languages that he doesn't even recognize: *"Salve o popolo d'eroi / Salve o patria immortale / Sono rinati I figli tuoi."* He doesn't mind not having shoes and underwear. After all, revolutionaries/highway robbers/pirates seldom wore them. Beds can also be dispensed with if one is willing to curl up in a corner and cover oneself with straw.

Wolf, on the other hand, collapses into a state of intense moroseness and paranoia (something always near the surface in his case). The weapons worry and frighten him. He envisions all sorts of accidents, blood everywhere, the last room filling up with more and more possessions (without them, with no one to put a halt to them – or worse, with someone else enjoying them). Or slowly being covered with dust, an archaeological display for the benefit of future inhabitants. Perhaps suicide would be the best: a single bullet ripping through both of them. Only, who would pull the trigger? He would, of course. He is the only one who can be trusted. Amil would move out of the way at the last moment. They'd have to fight over the honour of pulling the trigger. A combat in the heroic style. Wolf in loincloth, the knife gripped tightly between his teeth; Amil in military uniform, slapping the cudgel against his open palm. No matter how romantic such thoughts appear in the abstract, they always turn ugly – and dangerous – when the details are worked out.

These are the conditions at the time a singular event takes place to throw everything off-kilter, to begin an entropic cascade. Wolf, in the hope of at last coming up with a definitive explanation for the appearance and disappearance of the articles and out of fear that Amil might become violent, invites a librarian friend to come up to the room and participate in one of the searches. When Amil takes Wolf aside and demands an explanation for this strange female's presence, Wolf informs him that, aside from Basha's book cataloguing, she dabbles in astrology and telepathy and the study of signs. But this is unheard of, Amil whispers, casting a dubious glance at the imposing woman who stands with hands on hips, nose haughtily in the air. You can't bring someone else in here, he hisses. It's supposed to be just the two of us. Too late, Wolf says with an oily smile. I already have. And, unlike you, this is one person who can carry on a decent conversation. Wolf turns his back and walks away towards the librarian-astrologer. Amil looks at him for a moment, fists clenching, then slinks off to sit in his private corner.

Wolf, busy being garrulous with his new-found friend, ignores him. After a brief conversation about her name, which she says means "Daughter of God," the two sit down and begin their search in earnest, marking down what they find on the list and checking it against the previous night. Until that is, Basha comes across the tightly stretched, translucent table-lamp covering. Her reaction, a jumping back as if the covering were about to wrap itself around her, has Wolf scratching his head. *What is that?* she asks, having trouble catching her breath and with one hand across her throat. *How dare you...* She takes another deep breath. *You lured me in here to show me...that.* No, no, no, Wolf says. I just wanted to show you how things appear and disappear. *You're sick*, she says. *You're both sick in the head. Sick fucks. I'm going to call the police. You can't have things like that...* But, but, but, Wolf says, picking up the lamp and holding it out towards her. It's just a table lamp. Tomorrow, it'll be gone. *You hear that, God?* She looks up to the ceiling. *Just a table lamp, he says. The police, I tell you. They'll know what to do with you.*

Basha takes a step towards the door. Wolf reaches for her coat sleeve while blubbering that it is all a misunderstanding. That it is all Amil's fault. That if she doesn't like table lamps she just has to wait and it'll vanish. No problem. Silly old lamp. Basha pushes him away, sending him across the room. Wolf stumbles to the floor. *You'll be sorry. There are laws against this.* She turns and reaches for the door handle. As she does so, Amil springs up, shouts: Long live the squadristi! and hits her across the back of the head with the cudgel. With exactly the amount of force needed to stun but not kill her.

Amil drops the cudgel. Turning, he follows Wolf who is circling the edge of the room. Wolf stops and looks back at him. But neither sees the other. Instead, Wolf sees a pile of human bones that keeps growing, that keeps swallowing the space around it; Amil sees a series of identical men, naked, skeleton-thin, squatting painfully over chamber pots, the diarrhea pouring out of them like fetid, stagnant water. Killer! Wolf and Amil scream at the same time before lunging at each other.

Assassino! Amil shouts.

Attentäter! Wolf retorts.

A noise from near the entrance makes them hold up. Still somewhat stunned, Basha is trying to crawl away, reaching up for the door handle with one hand and clutching a purse with the other. She is muttering: *Please God, not again. Don't let it happen again. Help me...*

8

I'm sorry, Wolf says, smiling and offering her his hand. My friend has emotional control problems. Prone to outbursts. Neglected childhood and all that.

I'm prone to outbursts, Amil says. That's a good one. What happened the last time?

Please...

Oh, come on, Wolf says with a dismissive wave. That doesn't count. You heard what he called himself. A Marxist-Leninist of all things. You know how those guys make my blood boil.

Please...

Yeah, well, Amil says, you didn't have to shove his head in the oven.

Please...I...

What's she saying? Wolf asks, leaning down. What are you whispering?

As he places his ear near Basha's mouth, she pulls out a can from her purse and sprays him in the face. He screams and falls to the ground, fists rubbing against his eyes.

Amil tries to approach but she holds out the can menacingly.

Come closer, you bastard. You sick fuck. Come on. I dare you. There's plenty more where that came from. After I'm through with you, the cops will just have the mopping up. Unlike my ancestors, I'm not going like a lamb to slaughter.

Amil looks around, spots the gun where he's left it in his private corner. But before he can reach it, she backs out of the door and slams it shut behind her, all the while shouting: *Not again. Never again.*

Wolf continues to writhe. Amil locks the door and then squats beside him.

My eyes, Wolf says moaning. I can't see.

There is hammering on the door, followed by shouts to open it or have it broken down.

We have to leave, Amil says.

He leads Wolf towards the trunk, opens the lid and helps him to get in.

You should have killed her when you had the chance, Wolf says.

Yes, Amil says, lowering himself into the trunk and pulling shut the lid just as the front door smashes open. Maybe next time, I will.

EXORCISM

When he first stepped into the house, the owners ignored him completely. They had no wish for him to be there; or they'd changed their minds; or they simply couldn't see him – in the beginning it made little difference. The fact remained he was ignored. Mother, father, son and daughter, all moved daily towards their appointed rounds without being in the least disturbed by or interested in the strange man who had slipped in one night, all a-sweating, through a window left open on the ground floor. It discomfited the guest, however, since he had arrived with their letter of invitation in his hand and had knocked long and hard on the door before spotting the curtains billowing through the window. Unfortunately, before he could present himself properly, the letter was stolen or misplaced in the turmoil that followed his entrance. But he remembered very well what had been written on it: "You, _____, are cordially invited to marry our daughter on a day and time of your convenience and choosing. Till then, our home is yours. Please, make yourself welcome."

Well, it so happened this daughter acted most distant of all. While the rest of the family at least had the decency to sit down to breakfast with him, even if they didn't acknowledge his presence, she insisted on having hers in one of the numerous bedrooms sprinkled about the house. Occasionally, he would spot her approaching, dirty dishes in hand, from one end of the hall while he was at the other. He would rush to greet her, smiling and open-armed. But, between one blink and the next, she was gone (as if playing hide-and-seek with someone else). From a distance, from the distance she kept between them, she looked extraordinarily beautiful, almost translucent – and certainly what would have once been described as a "catch." And he could see no reason why he, rather than the various and sundry strangers that milled about the grounds, had been asked to marry her. This disparate crowd grew daily in size and was constantly underfoot. When the house was bulging and could take no more, they started to pitch tents on the vast expanse of lawn. They were, to a person, impeccably dressed and carrying expensively wrapped gifts. They were also all male. He concluded the family recognized male relations only. Or the daughter wanted to maintain a homogeneous coterie of friends and these were actually the wedding guests. He even made a game of trying to pick out who the best man was, assuming there was one. This was a thankless exercise as any of the hundreds could fit the bill – so close were they in dress, manner and attitude.

The truth was that, before receiving their letter, he had hardly given marriage a thought. Why he'd responded to their invitation remained a mystery. Curiosity? The lure of wealth and a name steeped in mystique? Through an examination of their records (open for all to see), he discovered the family was rich from undisclosed sources and owned the land for miles around. He wasn't greedy but a parcel of his own wouldn't be at all bad. In fact, having never owned more than the clothes on his back, he was of the opinion he deserved everything they gave him. This was negated nicely by the initial phase of silence with which he'd been greeted.

He spent the nights lying on his bed, asking himself questions. These questions served only to agitate him further as he could come up with no answers. The days began with meticulous searches through his pockets – he was always losing something; they ended with frantic explorations through the complex of rooms. Most, especially those occupied by the people he had come to call the wedding guests, were barely furnished, unpainted, harshly lit, with gyprock and ceiling beams showing. A few – always empty – were quite ornate, decorated with what he surmised were the sentimental jokes of the family: pictures of mythical animals, rosy-cheeked cupids, scenes from 19th-century melodrama. One day, he stumbled into what must be the wedding room. It was designed in the style of a miniature Sistine Chapel, complete with the story of the Creation and Fall of Man and ringed by rose-shaped stained-glass windows through which flowed a gorgeous flood of light. He knew this was no natural light but one stimulated through modern technology. Nevertheless, it felt like a holy place and something gently bowed his head. The slight pressure might have kept him in that position for the rest of the evening if a spider hadn't scuttled down from the ceiling (from between that tiny space that separates God's finger from Adam's) to play near his face. On another occasion, he overheard scattered bits of conversation from a room he happened to be passing. Female voice: "…can't touch it…" Male voice: "No…not any longer…" Female voice: "But it's…so beautiful…don't want to…" Male voice: "…must. For the family…" At this point, having either overheard him in turn or come to a natural conclusion, they ended the conversation and he tiptoed away not to risk being dis-covered.

Although the verbal silence between him and the family was never broken (except with the daughter), a type of communication did evolve. This was in the form of notes attached to his door. The first was signed by the father and read: "Love is an unnatural state of mind. I detest mixed marriages." Neither applied to him. Love might be a twitch in his genitals but never a state of mind and, as far as he could tell, they were of the same colour, race, religion and language. Yet, the note seemed particularly appropriate. The next day, an anonymous note: "Without love and without hope…" That was all. Followed by a threatening note from the brother: "You've caused us nothing but misery and sorrow. There is no reason for this. My sister is a fragile bird whose body has never been touched and whose heart beats pure. What about yours? I'll pray for the surgical return of your purity." A note from the mother: "I want your love. Without your love, I live in a world of quiet despair. My legs ache to think of your strong and delicate muscles pumping against me. Please come again."

He attempted at first to answer these with notes of his own, notes which he left scattered about the house. They went untouched. Perhaps they were glanced at, even read, but he couldn't be sure. In any case, he wasn't very good at writing and it took only the slightest hint of laughter, a suggested wisp of a smirk, to discourage him. This was the laughter, the smirk he interpreted behind the gesture of not accepting his notes. So, one evening, he gathered them all and threw them into the incinerator. A flurry of messages followed, littering the front of his door. Then they stopped. The wait was agonizing. He had expected naturally to advance from notes to civil conversation. Sign language, at least. Instead…a return to silence.

After not seeing them for several weeks, he found all four accidentally in a new attic he'd been exploring. He spotted them the moment he opened the trap door and poked his head in. They were hanging, not ten feet away, from the sturdy centre beam. He went no closer for, as much as he admired the dead in theory, he had no use for them first-hand. So he backed out and ran to his room. There, behind the safety of the abstract, he decided to solve the mystery. Taking out a piece of paper, he wrote four headings: Murder, Suicide, Accidental Death, Of Natural Causes.

• Murder: no motive; no weapon; no suspects (except the thousands of wedding guests and myself). The guests are out due to the very nature of their being here; the investigator is never a suspect.

• Suicide: very improbable; difficulty of accomplishing same; no reasons for such behaviour on their part. Is suicide a family affair?

• Accidental Death: my philosophy instructs me there is no such thing. All thoughts in this category will be shifted to the first and second.

• I conclude, therefore, by a process of elimination, that the four members of this family died, at the end of a long and productive life, Of Natural Causes which, being natural, couldn't be helped.

Naturally, the house was his. He would burn it down. But, first, he had to bury them. Perhaps they had a burying room, as well as a hanging room. He returned reluctantly to the attic, hoping the process of decomposition hadn't started yet. Climbing out of the trap door, he sniffed the air. Musty, but not putrid. Good, the flies and rodents hadn't yet discovered them. As he got up his courage to cut them down, a rope snapped and a body fell to the ground – head rolling off in one direction, the rest in another. He clutched at his stomach and threw up noisily into the fibreglass insulation. It was while wiping his mouth that he noticed the pieces of straw jutting out of the body's shirt-collar. Caught in the inertia of anger, he tore them apart, bit by bit, leaving the daughter for the last. Her, he raped – symbolically, at least. Then, sweeping up the leavings into a pile, he urinated and defecated on them.

This is the last straw, he said to himself as he climbed down out of the attic (and not getting his unintended pun). He was determined to leave them forever. Laugh at him, would they? He'd show them. But, first, he had to wash the spittle from his face. He opened the door to the toilet in his room, took one step in search of the light switch and plunged screaming into nothing. His tell-tale hand on the door knob saved him from plummeting into what he was sure was their bottomless room. He struggled to climb out and crawled back to his own room. It was only when he fell onto the bed that he noticed the stain spreading across the front of his trousers.

He slept for what seemed forever but which was actually two days. During that time, they took the opportunity to add innumerable rooms to the house. They also removed his clothes and replaced them with a wedding outfit, a spiffy grey tux that had been impeccably tailored. The tent guests were brought inside to join the others already in the house. They were installed in the pews according to some mysterious ranking and size of gift. Among them was a priest. He gawked at the replica Sistine Chapel (giving Eve the *mal'occhio*) and rubbed his hands appreciatively. A red carpet led from the bridegroom's door to the wedding room. There was no chance of his getting lost. Gifts lay scattered in the halls, mostly useless items: bird calls and eagle feathers and the occasional lizard in a glass cage.

When the bridegroom finally awoke from a dream of whores, he knew right away it was his wedding day. All the troubles of the previous weeks (silence, notes, practical jokes) came together, formed a heap on his chest. For some reason, there was now no turning back. When one builds to a climax, there's no sense in omitting it. By then, it's too late. ("Never too late; always too late," his mother relished saying over the phone.) He remembered as he dressed that no one from his family had been invited. And they had wanted so much to be there for his wedding, to make up for all the elopements. Perhaps it wouldn't seem this strange if they were there. Family has a way of destroying all mystery.

The first people he saw on opening the wedding-room door were his mother and father. What a surprise! They were talking in animated whispers to the bride's parents. How he would have liked to be playing with his mother's breasts at that moment. Of course, they all turned when he entered – his parents, the bride's parents, the brother, the priest, the rows upon rows of men. His mother crinkled her eyes; his father hoisted his pants with pride. Several of the guests put away their dice; others released a torrent of frogs; still others added grease to their hair. Radiant, unperspiring faces followed his progress to the altar. Arriving, he shook hands with his future father-in-law. He wavered a moment between shaking hands and kissing before leaving a print of his lips on his future mother-in-law's cheek. She turned and kissed him passionately, slipping her tongue into his mouth quickly back and forth, then biting him on the lip. The photographer snapped a picture but, in his hurry, cut off their heads. They were about to grapple, to take advantage of the heat of the moment, when the music started and they reluctantly separated.

The bride entered on the arm of her brother (who had taken the opportunity to sneak out). He didn't recognize her as the girl who continually avoided him. This one was solid, opaque. As she came towards him, the appropriate music was piped in through loudspeakers. But, when she reached him and had taken her position beside him, the person playing started shifting between tender waltzes and martial airs. This bothered no one except the bridegroom who was easily influenced by music. At one moment he stared dreamily into space; the next found him in the fixed-bayonet throes of patriotism.

(The brother: "It was I. I led her to the double-bladed axe. A creature never touched except by my unsullied hands. I watched her being penetrated before a crowd of dice-throwers. Then they gorged themselves for our benefit, running about the tents, chasing the animals, poking at each other with sharp sticks. One of them stumbled down the bottomless room. That helped make up for all the suffering and sacrifices. Most are gone now. Such banal relations he possesses. Illiterates that stink of the trough. No regard for art. No awareness of their meaningless lives.")

(Again, the brother: "I don't think I'll be able to listen to their night noises. Several times I have pleaded with my sister to stop, to halt the degeneration into a rutting bitch, but she's on his side now. In fact, the noises seem to have grown louder lately. Perhaps to spite me. My parents have settled into sullen gloom. They accuse *me* of allowing *her* to abandon *them*. How quickly they forget. I was against it from the beginning. And I told them he'd only dilute the blood of the family. But they wouldn't listen. By all rights, she should have been my bride. I was the only one fit for her.")

The silence deepened after the wedding. Except for the girl, of course, who took to talking all the time (even when he sweated and grunted to climax; even when she lowered her head onto his penis). She told him about the house and its rooms, the family, the silence, the notes, the practical jokes, the bottomless room, the wedding room, the things stolen, her brother, the guests rented in town, the addition of rooms, the deletion of rooms, the empty rooms, the unfurnished rooms, her body, her face, her fantasies, her innermost feelings. Then she questioned him about his house and his family, his face, his body, his feelings, his dreams. Did he masturbate? How often? Which fingers of which hand did he use? Would he do it in front of her? Was he in love with his mother? Her mother? Did he dream of being violated? Yet, while all this talking filled him with facts, new ideas and a sensation of being wanted, it didn't help clear up the confusion he'd felt from the moment he'd first climbed into that open window.

To escape the chatter and to give himself a chance to think, he resumed his daily tours of the house, which had continued to expand since the wedding. Occasionally, he still found a stranger or two lost in the maze of rooms. Invariably, they were emaciated and in need of psychiatric attention. He gave them soup and the name of a good mental hospital, then bundled them off. He also boarded up the door to the bottomless room, fastening iron bars across it. That didn't stop the strange scratching noises but at least gave the impression of neutralizing his fear.

Of the other three inhabitants, he saw less and less. They avoided him, no longer came down for breakfast, slammed doors in his face. But he didn't care for he was taking over more and more. The family obviously sensed this. They moved off to the corner of the house as far as possible removed from where he stayed. When he entered their room one day (purely by accident), they scurried about packing what they could carry and went in search of another home. The girl cried for a while, especially when she came across something or other that had belonged to one of them or reminded her of them. But he was happy to be alone and sole master of the mansion.

That didn't last long. The next day, while he was lifting her skirts in the grass outside the house, all but the few rooms that had been there from before his arrival collapsed into a red powder. The lizards, the mice, the birds, the spiders scattered into the fields. In their midst was some indescribable creature that left burn marks where it passed. When he saw this creature, he stood up but had to quickly sit down again because of vertigo. There, before him, like a slice of darkness in the ground, was a huge hole down which the red powder slowly sank.

He developed an aptitude for silence.

THE PHOTOGRAPHER
IN SEARCH OF DEATH

Kosmo, his boss at International Darkrooms Ltd., called him into the main office, away from the scurrying of minions who carried dusty folders from one section of the building to the other. Kosmo had his back to Quetzal but his pensive face reflected in the tinted window that covered one entire wall. Before him on the desk, opened at the last page, was a large black photo album, the old-fashioned kind with fancy little edges into which pictures could be fitted, pictures reproduced from film. No digital files need apply, the album stated. Quetzal was busy admiring its gloss when the entire building trembled and Kosmo swivelled about. His fingers were stained with silver nitrate and his deep-set eyes surrounded by lines and shadows.

"As you well know," he said with an accent that demanded respect, that was definitely not local, "you're my best photographer. The rest range from dilettantes to incompetents, from snap-happy digital cretins to cellphone starlets. You've filled most of the pages in this album."

Quetzal felt light-headed with pride, pleased to have been singled out. And for having his love of old technology valorized. The floor shook beneath him. Across the road, a ledge gave way, plummeting to the ground below.

"Now, I have one last assignment before I leave for my high-country villa, an assignment only you can carry out." He paused for a moment and stared intently at the album. "I want a photograph of death to complete this album. That's it. I don't think I need to give you further instructions."

He looked up at Quetzal, stained fingertips touching, hooded eyes brooding, then swivelled to continue his quiet scanning of the city, a city coming apart at the seams.

International agreed – without bickering – it should pay all Quetzal's expenses. The first thing he did was to arm himself with the latest-model SLRs (there was a limit to his Luddite tendencies) and accessories from the company stockroom, as well as film that was "guaranteed to capture the most minute of details and not become grainy under normal conditions."

But, never before having thought of capturing death on film, what he needed most was practice in getting the concept right. All his best photographs had been done that way – with the realization it's not the snap of the shutter that counts but the preparation that went into the shot. Gatta, the woman who for the last few months had shared the small basement apartment with him, volunteered to pose and together they converted his place into a temporary funeral parlour. Gatta put on a scratchy recording of Bach's "Suite No. 1 for Cello Solo" and then covered the bed – the only piece of furniture in the room – with a red comforter. Finally, she lay down and folded her large bony hands so as to form a cross on her scrawny chest. Quetzal, in a moment of inspiration, pushed one of Gatta's plastic flowers between them.

He milled about the inert, seemingly unbreathing body, quickly arranging camera angles and lighting. Between tremors and cascades of dust, he snapped his photos. On his mimed instructions, Gatta stripped so that he could capture the extreme whiteness of her skin, always pale and horribly lacking in blood. Each shot – especially those taken with the 4-by-5 portrait camera – proved a marvel of technical perfection. He hung the finished prints to dry along the cracked walls, next to a faded hieroglyph depicting a stylized corn stalk. While Gatta applauded his skill by rubbing herself against him and keeping up a constant chatter, he sat on the bed musing.

"The stillness isn't there," he said at last, letting a print float lazily to the ground.

Quetzal turned off the record player, then opened his only window with some difficulty. It was narrow and triangular in shape, no more than a foot high in all. Soon, he thought, it would become impossible to open. Or close. The prints flapped back and forth as the dusty wind picked up. Gatta took his hand and began to kiss his fingers one by one, licking the webbing between them, sucking the tips. He continued to stare out at the remnants of sky-scrapers in the distance, jagged like rotten teeth in a crone's mouth. A blackbird settled gently onto a light cable – and was charred to a crisp.

"No. The stillness definitely isn't there. I have to go out. Don't wait for me."

The brisk autumn weather forced Quetzal to wear his down-lined coat and a long-striped scarf, the one that had been knitted by his mother while in the hospital. The far end was unfinished since she had died suddenly (of heartbreak, she claimed with her dying breath) after making a miraculous recovery from a combination of breast, lung and cervical cancer. He had to be careful it didn't unravel completely on him. In her zeal to keep him warm, Gatta wrapped the scarf too tightly about his neck. He loosened it and, shouldering several different format cameras, went in search of death. Gatta stayed behind, not insisting but nevertheless convinced her version was infinitely better than the real thing. She kept a bag permanently packed under the bed but had no intention of leaving. For the moment.

As Quetzal walked along the cracking, undulating streets, he admitted to being frightened. Certainly, not of death, no. He knew, however, this was the most important assignment of his life.

Kosmo was obviously testing him for still more valuable tasks. His personal photographer, perhaps, in charge of recording him for posterity. Landscapes or Portraitures at the very least, sketching the beauty of the sylvan valley surrounding his protected highland villa.

And, if he bungled it, he would have no one to blame but himself. Death – or rather its most impressive representatives, dead people – could be found on almost every corner. Sections of the city were completely cut off from water, gas, electricity; some parts even physically with wide chasms plunging deep into the bowels of the earth. Hourly, new tremors were set off, slicing open everything in their path. Those who could afford to had left for the countryside – and safety – long before it had come to this. Only the poor, the indifferent, the trapped remained, living in the few reasonably safe places – the cellars that had been uncovered in excavation, the cellars built long before the skyscrapers, their walls a reddish clay imbedded with what seemed shards of pottery and broken figurines.

Of late, the tremors and the subsequent opening up of the city's intestines had attracted the interest of archaeologists from around the world. Everywhere could be heard the beating of propellers, the whipping up of choking dust as the helicopters carrying them swooped in to land. And they swarmed out, hard hats on, wading knee-deep through the shells of collapsed structures, their delicate brushes sweeping away even the tiniest speck of dust from newly raised artifacts.

A bone fragment here, the tip of an antique rattle there. Quetzal admired the way they were able to reconstruct a city beneath the city with these bits and pieces. The speculation ran rampant. According to the latest cluster of theories, the lower half, the half below the street-line, was in actual fact the remnant of an ancient civilization which had migrated or been driven north.

Naturally they believed in human sacrifice of some form or other and these were the victims' bones being discovered since the dominant culture indulged in cremation.

"Why would anyone in their right minds," Gatta had asked in her mock-quizzical manner, "want to migrate north from that warm, sunny place?"

Quetzal had shrugged and looked once again at the hieroglyph on his wall, as if this time illumination would come. He had spent many hours at the library on account of it, risking the most tremor-riddled portion of the city. But he never got any further than the rather obvious fact it was the representation of a corn stalk, stylized and angular, a corn stalk gone to seed.

A platoon of eager archaeologists, all wearing the insignia of the Lost Wax Corp., was busy reconstructing what moments before had been a rare book store with a set of apartments above it. They dusted clean a group of skeletons, squatting in unnatural ways around the petrified remains of a low tree trunk. Above them, hanging from a balcony and completely ignored, were the bodies of the building's latest occupants. Quetzal slipped into the wreckage and began taking pictures, first of the skeletons and then of the bodies. A piece of string dangled from a child's pocket, his foot caught in a balcony railing. Quetzal couldn't help himself. He reached over and pulled on it. The child's sweater fell apart in slow-motion. A scowling archaeologist shook his fist at the photographer and told him to get out, the area was out of bounds for civilians. Quetzal, overjoyed at having found death so quickly, paid no heed. Something flew by his head and exploded behind him. The archaeologists had set aside their brushes and were advancing on him with shovels held high. He scrambled away, still snapping wildly as he backed out of the excavation site.

"I have it!" Quetzal yelled, using his shoulder to force open the door to his apartment.

He hurried to embrace Gatta who was sprawled on the bed with one of her many swarthy lovers – and almost choked when his scarf caught on a shard.

"I have it!" he cried in a falsetto.

He released himself from the scarf's stranglehold and quickly set to work in the tiny room he used for developing his prints. This room had been excavated to a level even below that of the base-ment-suite to protect it from any hint of light whatsoever. It was damp and fungoid and full of pale, translucent creatures that scut-tled in the corners, but Quetzal worked cheerfully. On the bed, Gatta and her gaunt-eyed friend made desultory love, spurred on by the increasing tempo of the tremors that added new crevasses by the minute. Then, entwined, the two fell asleep. Gatta opened her eyes when Quetzal emerged in the middle of the night, the dis-appointment etched on his face like the ever-widening cracks on the street. Placed side by side with her poses, the shots of the fam-ily could hardly be distinguished.

"I told you," Gatta said gently, gobbling up a bowl of cottage cheese, milk and bread and following it up with a bottle of beer which she waved about as she spoke.

"Death isn't there. Everyone's faking it just to get sympathy. Tell what's-his-name to stuff it tight up you-know-what."

She ushered her lover out of the house, giving him one last, deep tongue-to-tongue kiss. Quetzal absent-mindedly took his place on the bed – right on the lover's indentation – and lay mus-ing with his arms spread out over his head.

"It's my fault, not the camera's."

Gatta wiped her mouth and eased herself down beside him. Her head was against his waist; her long legs dangled over the edge of the bed. That's how they fell asleep.

Quetzal returned to International Darkrooms the next day for instructions and guidance only to find the entire building one gigantic pile of rubble. Truckloads of archaeologists pored over the site and sheets of photographic paper blackened in the sun. Kosmo and his photo album were gone. No one could tell him if the boss had escaped or had been swallowed up. Quetzal had wanted to ask him for an extension. He considered it granted.

With the ever-increasing state of confusion in the city and the migration of better qualified personnel, Quetzal was able to secure a job as a male nurse for a man dying of leukemia. The stricken man lived by himself on the outskirts of the city – his wife having left the moment the diagnosis had been made – and he welcomed a suggestion to have Gatta reside there as well. He fell in love with her "alabaster skin" the moment he laid eyes on her, and Quetzal saw to it the two of them slept together whenever they desired.

In no time, that was a nightly occurrence.

Quetzal discharged his duties honestly and with tender care. Each day, he washed the man thoroughly and fed his emaciated frame. Each day, until the wretched fellow was no longer able to stay on his feet, he walked with him around the walled-in garden.

Afterwards, they sat, all three, under the central sycamore tree and talked. The man said he was an author of some renown and had written dozens of books on any subject that came to mind – from knitting to strange customs. Quetzal or Gatta wiped his mouth when he dribbled, something he was prone to do when lost in his flights of fancy.

But, no matter how much Quetzal wished him to remain as he was, frozen perhaps at a certain moment between sickness and health, the man weakened daily as the white blood cells in his body multiplied unchecked, fighting a phantom disorder. Gatta persisted in sleeping with him to the very end, allowing him every considerable pleasure of which she was capable. Quetzal would often come in to perform some menial duty and find them struggling with each other beneath the blankets.

After several months, the man became bedridden, hardly able to shift about on the huge king-size mattress that made him look even more shrivelled, even more childlike. A week later, he summoned Quetzal by means of the bell at the head of his bed. He was sitting up, pillows supporting his head, a thin arm tightly about Gatta who sat beside him.

"Tomorrow," he said, in a reedy voice barely above a whisper, "is my birthday. My thirty-third birthday. You know what that means? I want you to gather up all my papers and flush them down the toilet. Will you do that?"

Quetzal nodded and returned to his own room, settling down to wait for the death rattle. He was certain it would come that night. As he listened to the springs sounding in the dying man's room, tears streamed from his eyes. His clothes were soaked with perspiration. He placed a finger across his heart and listened to its insistent beat. He felt nothing could still it. All night long, he alternated between the death vigil and moments of half-sleep. But the morning came and nothing happened.

Gatta rose out of bed long enough to freshen up and help Quetzal bake a cake. The three sang "For He's a Jolly Good Fellow." Gatta and Quetzal danced a bit while the dying man clapped his hands feebly and made gurgling noises. Then he fell asleep.

Quetzal took the opportunity to search through his dressers and commodes. He found sheet upon sheet covered with geometric designs – triangles in particular – and the design of a man in a conical cap, surrounded by bright feathers and the abstract heads of animals, leopards and snakes in particular. These seemed to have been photocopied endlessly, filling whole drawers. Quetzal gathered the papers in his arms and was about to dispose of them when the man awoke.

"What are you doing!" he cried hysterically, his voice a loud squeak, a look of absolute horror on his face. "Put those back!

What are you doing with my papers? I didn't mean it. It was only a joke. Put those back or I'll have you arrested. Police! Police! He's trying to kill me!"

Gatta smothered his face with kisses, pushed her breasts against his lips, half-shoving them into his mouth. This gave Quetzal the opportunity to flush the papers bit by bit down the toilet. The man struggled pathetically each time he heard the water running, but Gatta was irresistible. Her body provided clean blood for him and an unnatural warmth. Quetzal examined the room several times to make sure he had carried out his orders fully. He found another cache under the bed. The man blubbered well into the afternoon. Each time Gatta released him to catch her breath or to relieve the rawness between her legs, he would start gesturing with his hands as if drawing in air.

Quetzal slept well for most of that night, a dreamless, dark sleep in a cool, mushroomy room. The next morning, with the sun half-risen, he was jolted awake by a sharp thud against the adjoining wall. Another followed as he was about to sink back into sleep. He threw on a robe and rushed into the room. Gatta shivered beside the dying man although thick blankets covered her. She tried to say something but the words dribbled down her chin. The dying man lay unperturbed, his hand fastened to Gatta's. Quetzal sobbed. He couldn't bring himself to raise the camera to his eye. Especially since the dying man had taken the opportunity to fix him with his own eye, had nailed him right through the heart.

"Quetzal… Quetzal," Gatta mumbled. "Please. I can feel him. I can…"

A tremor shook Quetzal into frenzied activity. He pulled the red blanket off the bed, revealing the two naked bodies attached beneath, and set up his twin-lens portrait camera. When that didn't totally satisfy him, he climbed onto the bed itself and straddled both Gatta and the dead man. All the while, leaping from position to position, he kept wiping his eyes with the back of his hand. Gatta fought half-heartedly to release herself from the man's grip, attempting at one point to pry him loose one finger at a time.

"Keep pulling at him!" Quetzal yelled. "Keep tugging! Let's see a bit of fear in those beautiful black eyes! He's dying; he's dead; to a bleached corpse you'll be wed!"

Gatta tumbled out of bed, dragging the light-as-a-feather man behind her like papier mâché. She pushed at his chest, kicked at his head without the least sign of emotion, causing a long gash across his mouth. But there was no letting go and, surrendering at last to the inevitableness of his hold, she knelt down beside him and started kissing his body.

Quetzal, with death squarely in his sights, had no intention of being interrupted. An objective observer, he followed the struggles with interest, choosing with a professional eye the best framing, lighting, composition, etc. He took close-ups and wide-angle shots, portions of bodies and bedposts, time-lapse studies and flights of fancy. It was only after running out of film that he helped Gatta get loose, prying his fingers apart. She didn't move but continued to kneel with the dead man's arm straddling her thigh. Quetzal threw the red blanket on her. Then, folding the dead man's arms across his chest, he picked him up and carried him to the bed. Gatta curled up on the floor, knees up against her chin. Deep tremors shook loose a portrait of the man's wife. The glass splintered around her smile. Gatta pulled spasmodically at the loose threads on the blanket. She started at one corner and pulled till she reached the other.

Quetzal removed the film from his cameras and then smashed them against the walls. He lifted Gatta up into his arms. She was a dead weight, not making the least effort to ease his load. Her fingers threaded furiously at the blanket, leaving strands of wool in her wake.

Back at the centre of the city, archaeologists flooded the streets, shouting after each discovery, bolder with each passing moment, dusting off anyone or anything that stood still. Tremors were constant now, opening up wrinkle-like cracks beneath their safety boots. Occasionally, some would fall in but that was considered a necessary risk and they were given a brisk burial service. Quetzal kicked open the door to his room after several tries and settled Gatta gently on the bed. She continued unravelling the blanket, denuding herself in the process. Then, having finished with that, she wrapped the scarf about herself and went to work on it.

Quetzal spent the entire night in his darkroom, puzzling over the intricacies of development. He took special care with his solutions. Everything was worked out to the least detail, especially in the processing of the film. Test sample followed test sample till he had exactly the right paper, the right lighting, the right cropping angles.

And, finally, much to his surprise, he realized – in the otherworldly glow of the darkroom light – that he had succeeded in capturing the look of death. He came rushing out to show Gatta but none of the lights in the room worked. Only the moonlight through the window made it possible to see.

At least a sixty-second exposure, he thought. At least sixty seconds. He floated to the window and tried to pry it open. It was stuck. A man in a conical cap strolled by. Quetzal turned to Gatta, waving a wet print in her face.

"I've got to get this to Kosmo," he stammered in his excitement. "You wait here. It's dangerous on the streets."

And, kissing her on the cheek, he went out the door, the door that could no longer be closed, leaving behind him a woman on a bed surrounded by red threads as thick as worms.

START

There is a point at which one must start.

He started under the deep vault of a sky whose pinpricks resembled nothing so much as stars. He started as a doubling in a reflective surface. Naked. Eyes engorged to compensate for the poor lighting. On extending his hand, the palm of his hand, he could feel a cool wall, projecting up, arching and ribbed ever so slightly, but not breathing. Around him, floating through densely packed particles, the faces of chess pawns, the marbled faces set in their troubled expressions. When not in motion, they sat weighted on luminescent boards whose squares changed shapes upon being touched. These were scattered at head level about what, he suddenly realized, must be a room. Or some portion of a room. He moved one of the nearer pawns, lifting it and then lowering it gingerly on to a new square. But, the moment he took his fingers off the piece it sprang back, in a series of arcs and barely visible transitions, to its previous position. He tried this several times, always with the same result. In a rush of anger, he began to knock away the pawns, striking left and right, sending them tumbling, bouncing to the mirrored floor. They floated back to where they had been without a murmur of protest, without revealing the slightest discomfort. Serenely, as if he understood, he nodded and continued. Soon, the air thinned and he could see clearly the pinpricks twinkling far overhead – and underfoot. He watched himself kneel down to run his tongue along the veins of the marble. It was a blue tongue and had tasted much that made no sense. He licked the marble blindly, following the river that flowed just beneath its surface, till he came to the edge of something. An oval entrance. Upon looking out, he noticed everything was only half of what he had come to expect: sheared down the middle from firmament to foundation as if by some gigantic saw. Outside, there was nothing, a vast emptiness bereft of the least identifying mark, the least hint of gravity. Behind him, the half-room, the semi-domed vault where the thick air rolled towards him in waves, freezing all in its path: the lugubrious drinkers in pink cafés; the rats brushing their teeth; the strangers in the guest room. Soon, he knew, the temperature would drop to absolute zero, the morose intractable cold snuffing out even the thought of thought. But yet he couldn't move from the edge, for the edge was all there was. He turned to face the advancing wall, watching it fill the entire vault, watching it extinguish the pinpricks. It, too, was veined and mirrored and he could see himself being pushed back, back to the limit beyond which there was nothing. At the last moment, as he was about to plunge from the edge, toes holding the edge like some universal diver, he stuck out his blue tongue. It sizzled against the wall, sticking fast, and he dangled helplessly above the void, making whining noises, alive for a moment more, his bowels emptying, a stream of semen squeezed out of his shrunken testicles. And then his tongue snapped with the cold and he fell.

Or so he thought.

For there was really no falling. Rather a climbing, a swimming upwards, mouth full of blood and salt water, the cauterized stump of what might have been a blue tongue. Upwards, ever upwards in the dark, the lungs forming and then threatening to burst, the pectorals growing stronger with each breast stroke. Come, come, a voice seemed to call. There is magic awaiting you here. Come. Upwards, then, beyond claustrophobia, beyond the saline pressure, beyond the dream of consciousness and star systems. Upwards, then, not knowing the exact moment the surface of this world was pierced, emerging into a wetness with tangled roots and hot fetid breath and a tree that grew in layers of sentience, that took the limp body and sliced it open with its dead branches, violating it repeatedly till the feeling of her emerged. And she understood, shuddering, the unacceptable, snapping a twig from the spent tree. Thus, it fell upon her to sweep away the remnants, the last traces of the ache, knowing full well what it meant – that she alone kept the temperature slightly above absolute zero, that she alone had swum the empty distance, the gap between one edge and the next. For there were real stars glittering in the tree, not pinpricks, and it was towards those she started to climb, a branch at a time, stopping occasionally to look down at what had become a frozen sea below her, the waves solid, some reaching up like clenched fists in desperation. While still close to the ground, she could see the transparent creatures thrown up from the bottom, trapped, their huge eyes burnt away in the harsh sun; she could see the dolphins and the whisper of a child's breath; she could see a tiny tongueless shape emitting a halo of cracks that almost made it to the surface – but not quite. Not quite. And, as she climbed, her flesh brushed against the soft, furry bark and she was eyewitness to the shells left behind by creatures in a hurry. For there were limbs everywhere, torn in the fleeing. And kitchen utensils. And a book on matrix algebra. Telephones ringing, transmitting encoded data. On the higher levels, half-hidden by the foliage, entire banks of electronic circuits called out to be reactivated, some enticing her with screens upon which pawns on checkerboard patterns shifted constantly. But she didn't stop until she arrived at the top, poking her head through the oval aperture just as the tree crumbled to nothing beneath her and the hole sealed, healing itself of her invasion.

And she reasoned it instantly as her world: featureless, a metallic grey one moment; the next, tumescent with colour, full of crystal and alpha waves. The effort, the attempt to focus, caused it to change, to invert itself. Invariant was a glow on the horizon, like a semi-dome. She began to walk towards it, kicking aside the tiny plants that puffed into the air, bursting like miniature rainbows. And, walking, she didn't notice the edge of the buzz saw that sang in the sky above her, almost invisible on its side, held together by a furious energy – and that sliced her in half, clean across the middle, without feeling or pain. Just a cold gushing around her waist, the nerve endings retracting and a tiny bird that fluttered within her cupped hands, straining to get away. But she wouldn't let it go, clutched at it desperately as she tottered to the ground, legless, awaiting the vertical cut that would finish her off. It didn't come. Instead, a veined checkerboard floating nearby slid beneath and sizzled flat against her wound. And the nerve endings reached out like roots to imbed themselves, one by one, in the unyielding metal and the tiny bird, released at last, flew to safety. Truncated, she rose into the sky, tongue swelling in her mouth. But it wasn't her tongue alone, not hers alone. She felt a sharing with another half-creature whose pulse was directly opposite hers. No matter how hard she tried, however, she couldn't flip herself around to see with whom she was sharing. Only feel the duality: one moment, the stump of a tongue, the next, a slithering snake; one moment, an Amazon's breasts, the next, smooth Apollonian muscles; one moment, a deep damp cave full of life and sentience, the next, a worm's deadly eye.

And she twisted, alternating right-side up and upside down, swirling towards the horizon, watching the pinpricks pass directly overhead, marking the zenith, the other half of the room, the half-glow opening of flesh and metal.

And he twisted, alternating upside down and right-side up, swirling towards the horizon, watching the stars pass directly overhead, marking the zenith, the other half of the room, the half glow opening of metal and flesh.

It was then she lowered her arms and he lowered his and their fingers entwined. It was then the spark caused them to catch their breaths. It was then the world inverted again. It was then they realized they'd sucked all the air out of the universe.

It was then they wouldn't let go.

There is a point at which one must choose to end.

THE SAVIOUR

For as long as I can remember, I have watched you leave your house promptly at five in the morning (six mornings a week – on the seventh one rests naturally)…I have watched you leave your home with a shining aluminum lunch box in your left hand. And every morning, your first stop has been the decrepit corner store with its flickering neon sign and faded window displays of little kiddies sipping Coke. There, you've nodded at the unshaven owner – as decrepit as the store – and then have bought a news-paper from the rusted bin. You've always picked out the second paper. Never the first. On several occasions, I myself have bought the first and the third to see if there is any difference between them. I have discovered none. And, when you've left the store, looking neither left nor right, you've stepped immediately onto the bus that has taken you to work.

At this point, we've always parted ways and I don't see you again until your return in the evening, your face enveloped in a series of ever-increasing wrinkles. But these mustn't be mistaken for signs of worry. Or depression. You are a happy and uncon-cerned man, a constant whistler and smiler, delighted as much by the sight of worms after a heavy rain as by the first rose of the sea-son from your well-tended arbour. Bronzed as you are from your outside work, health fairly explodes from you, radiates outward to douse those fortunate enough to come near. Your only physical defect seems to be a pronounced squint that signals less than per-fect eyesight and the need for glasses.

So, partly out of pity (a profound pity) and partly out of self-interest (knowledge must be imparted – like a juicy apple – on those who lack it), I've decided to take you under my wing. No, this isn't a spur of the moment decision. As you gather, I've known you for a long time, observed you, hoped you'd eventually snap out of it and come to your senses like the rest of us. But you haven't and so I have no choice but to save you. No, no. It's all right. You have nothing to do but relax and let me save you. Surely that isn't much to ask of a long-time neighbour whom I feel I know as thoroughly as myself, as precisely as a digital watch, as completely as a syllogism.

First, just to make sure we understand each other, I set fire to your house in the middle of a clear cold night, the stars blinking crisply overhead, the snow crackling underfoot. You must know it's ridiculously easy setting fire to that neat, little box you call your domicile. You have a connecting wooden shed in the back that's filled with yellowing newspapers (all seconds, no doubt), cardboard boxes and dusty, oil-stained rags. After making sure the spark has caught and the flames are spiralling through the shed, glowing and hissing like a trail of wet snakes, I run around to the front and rap on your door – rap loudly and insistently, yelling at the top of my voice. I wouldn't want you to go up as well, curling brown around the edges, all bubbly and toasted like plastic. No, that wouldn't do. In fact, I even burst in to pull you out of bed, as you have no fire alarm and would soon go under, if not from panic then from smoke inhalation.

It's touch and go for a while as I race up the stairs, wet kerchief around my mouth, guided only by your coughing – that breathless hacking, hoping against hope it's not too late. I call out your name, grope for you, tell you there's no time to save anything. No, nothing at all. You must get out now before it's too late. And, wrapping a grey wool Hudson's Bay blanket about your shoulders, I lead you out into the street. Where you watch, poor destitute soul, the flames soaring crisply into the sky, reaching, reaching, their hot little fingers daring to singe the stars themselves. And you listen to the chopping of axes, the shouts of determined firemen, the gush of half-frozen water bursting through your apertures and out again, creating a miasmic wonderland. It is a wonderland, isn't it? A wonderland consisting of your possessions all strung together with mud and ashes.

But you're trembling, poor boy. You're literally shaking in your slippers. What to do? Of course! What you need is shelter, someplace to hang your head – even if only for awhile. How thoughtless of me not to offer sooner. My house is your house. *Mia casa e sua casa. Ma maison est votre maison.* Come, come. Turn your back on trouble. Forget the slick destruction that's done away with everything you owned, loved, felt for. I live, you know, right across the street. Well, a bit diagonally actually. And, wouldn't you know it, I just happen to have a spare bed in the guest room, all made up, the clean starched sheets folded back, pillows puffed out, with a goose-down duvet to keep out the chill. There, there, lie yourself down. I'll make you a nice cup of tea. Regular or camomile? Or would you prefer something stronger, a wee blast to stoke your own fizzling furnace, to remove a bit of that grey from your ashen face? Both? Why not? That's splendid.

I watch you, afterwards, asleep, curling into a tense, tight ball as if to offer the least possible surface to the hostile world. And I know that, only nodding acquaintances till now, we are sure to become, with a little luck and lots of good intentions, the best of friends. My house is yours, I say, for as long as you wish it, for as long as you need it. You're shy, I can tell. Worry about imposing, about getting in the way, about disrupting the "pattern of my life." Ah, what a considerate man! But I assure you there is room here enough for the two of us, room to expand, to grow. *Lebensraum*, I think they call it. It's a big house. Too big really for only one person. A house filled with a large family's ambience and the crippled dreams of my parents. Or was that the dreams of my crippled parents? Besides, where would you go in the middle of winter? The rents are steep and the flats bloated with cockroaches and undulating ice patches. Best to save your money. Yes, yes. If you insist. I can't complain if you buy a little food for the pantry, a little replenishment for the liquor cabinet.

For the next few weeks, your salvation goes well. You leave from my house at five in the morning, a brand-new shining aluminum lunch box in your left hand and a hard hat stuck firmly on your head. Ah, the determined warrior. And in the evening, the dishes done, the paper read, we play cards. Your deal. But, soon, I notice a restlessness, a vacant distant look in your eyes between the shuffle and the draw. I ask what is wrong. I ask perhaps you'd like to play a different game. You shake your head. This goes on for one, two, a whole slew of nights. Then one evening, on what might very well be the coldest evening of the year, you rise from the table, dress and go out, leaving me on the verge of certain defeat. I'm too flabbergasted to call out after you, to ask what it is I've done wrong. You return several hours later when I'm already in bed. I see the yellow light spill under my door. I listen to you creaking up the stairs. I hold my breath as the toilet flushes. But the lights go out and the door to your room slides silently shut.

The next evening I'm prepared — coat, hat, boots stacked neatly, hidden but ready to go. I give you a one-minute start, count it down meticulously, then follow. And where do you go? What hidden paths do you take? What secret vices do you indulge? Why, none at all, it seems. You head straight for the slovenly little store on the corner where a little girl runs on newly shined patent leather shoes and the neon flickers nastily — like sizzling bacon. This is where you go. This is what you do. Sit on a well-worn stool to discuss the horses, to banter about the lottery numbers, to sip cheap gin from a polystyrene cup. I wait outside, tears running down my cheeks, feeling immensely cold and immensely sorry for myself. But then I think: Why should I feel sorry for myself? It's you I should be feeling sorry for. It's you who resists the ultimate state of grace, the warm tender blanket of salvation.

So, I wipe my frozen tears and make my way home, knowing full well what I must do. I must eliminate the source of temptation. There's no escaping one's fate, no matter how much one dodges, lashes out, squirms away from the spotlight's vicious glare. I have been chosen to save you and if that entails killing a store owner, then so be it. Once decided, the actual task is ludicrously easy. The man takes no precautions; he drinks himself into a stupor; when the last customer leaves, he pulls open a trap door and jovially urinates into the dark hole; then he stumbles about turning off the lights, leaving only the frizzing neon, the sputtering relic, and locks the door behind him. He's a wheezer – bad heart, maybe or simply overweight. He falls around the corner of the building, holding on to the edge, and runs smack dab into me. "Oh hi," he sloshes, stumbling back. "It's you." "Hi," I say, and slip the steak knife through his dirty duffel coat between his ribs, into the centre of his heart. Then out again. He doubles over with a grunt, trying to get my attention by reaching out for my pant leg. But I can't have that and drive the knife into his throat, severing the jugular. His grunts turn to gurgles. Then silence. He twitches, shudders, stiffens and is dead. Yes, it's that simple, really. All that's left is for me to wipe the knife – on his filthy trousers.

But are you happy? Are you pleased with this turn of events? Of course not. You come home the following night pale and shaken. In a voice barely audible, you relate how the world is collapsing around you, how all the good, steady things are falling to pieces. What have I done to deserve this? you ask me. First my house goes up in flames (there's the shell diagonally across the street, a grisly reminder, as you say); now I find the corner store shuttered and learn the owner has been brutally murdered (for your own good, I whisper, but only to myself). What's that? The world's up to no good, I say. You continue: Where will I buy my paper now? Where will I go in the evening to talk? About horses? I suggest. Yes. About horses and other things. Curse the idiot for dying. How dare he leave me stranded. How dare he indeed, I say, all sympathy. Aren't you fortunate to have me, steadfast and true, ignoring repeated betrayal? I can't talk about horses but I can still be of comfort, I can still keep you from the blows of fate.

And so, I lead you to bed, undress you and tuck you in, confident your state of grace is fast approaching. It's like that first night, I think, with the fire roaring away. So it stays for the rest of the winter and well into spring. I have filled the house with games, from Scrabble to Chess to Go-Moku. We play them in the evening when you return from work. Or we go for walks through the local park, excited by the coming warmth, the lengthening days, the sturdy cement of friendship which no thaw can upheave or crack.

Or so it seems. For it is only seeming. It is only a preparation for further treachery, a ruse to keep me from recognizing the landscape of your cruelty. That blow comes on a hot August night as we sip homemade lemonade (only the best for Judas) in the backyard, waiting for the first stars to appear. There! I say excitedly. That's Venus! I've found a new place, you say. That's nice, I say. It's also the Morning Star, you know…I need a place of my own, you know, you say. It's my one chance. You can come and visit. You'll come to visit, won't you? Sure, I will, I say, sipping the last of the lemonade, appreciating its bitterness. Here's a toast to your new place. Phew, you say, I didn't know how to break it to you. I didn't think you'd take it so well.

The following morning, while you're on your way to work, I call the quarry where you've spent most of your days, hacking away at blocks of stone (much like you yourself). I call pretending to be you, imitating your voice so well, the foreman really believes it's you telling him he's a bastard and his parents were bastards and his wife's a dog who's made it with a brace of Fuller Brush salesmen. Well, I shouldn't be, but I'm feeling genuinely sorry when you return in the evening with a black eye and can't explain why your foreman suddenly tried to attack you with a shovel and was kept from bashing your brains in only by the intervention of the other men. Ah, now you break down in tears, do you? Now, you come running to me, crying on my shoulder. Life is cruel and confusing, isn't it? You can't understand what happened, why you were fired after so many years of faithful service, can you? And, dear oh dear, what'll become of you now? I mean, you obviously can't afford a place of your own. That's for sure. Don't worry, I say, patting your baby cheeks, your pink healthy skin. You can stay here for as long as you want. Really? you say. Oh, thank you. That's right, I think. That's right. Don't you worry. Leave me to do all the work – I'm used to it. So what if my face is gaunt and shrivelled? So what if I've a twitch that won't go away? So what if my legs are wobbly and, in my terrible confusion, I constantly mistake the Snakes for the Ladders.

What does it matter so long as you, my friend, are about to be saved, are only a few steps away from salvation? And it will not have been in vain. For you and I are going on a picnic. Tomorrow. Don't worry about packing. I'll take care of that. And I know just the spot, a park filled with childhood memories and oaks. A bit overgrown, perhaps, but that adds to the naturalness of it all. Besides, you wouldn't want one of those manicured lawn affairs overrun with brats and skimpy bathing suits. The sun is hot though, isn't it? Here, let's move beneath this lovely oak. I spread a purple blanket in the shade. We sit. Birds preen themselves; bees slither into golden flowers. I take out a bottle of fine red wine and pour two glasses. Let's toast. What shall we toast? I toast the ant crawling up your thigh; you drown it in a drop that balls up with dirt. Here, then. Here's a loaf of bread I rip apart with my own hands. Cheese, too. Ripe and crumbly. Oh dear, I think I have to shake a leg. I stand up and circle behind the tree. You take a sip of the wine, make some comment on its not lasting too much longer, especially in this heat. Then you talk of misfortune, the misfortune of your life – from the burning of your home to the losing of your job. From behind the tree, I pretend to urinate (making the noise with my mouth) while you continue talking, now thanking me for my generosity and kind-heartedness, for my saintly ability to forgive and forget. Not at all, I say, sneaking up behind you and pulling a noosed rope from the picnic basket. It snakes into the air. Before you can swallow even one bite of your thick piece of bread, I have it tight around your neck and looped over the lowest branch. Then, catching the other end before it hits the ground, I run as quickly as possible through the high grass, the prickly nettles, pulling you rudely but efficiently towards the sky. You kick and struggle, the bread vomiting itself into the air, a wetness spreading across the front of your trousers. Then, with one last jerk, I let go and you fall in a heap.

You gasp for lost breath and clutch at me when I kneel down beside you. Your eyes flutter up into your skull. Your tongue is cut almost in half. Your thighs quiver and spasm. The bruise about your neck slowly fills with red. I tilt your head up slightly towards me and allow you tiny sips of the wine. Oh dear. It's turned to vinegar. You scream when it touches your bloodied tongue. Now, now, I say, placing your head against my chest and rocking you. It's all right. I'm here to save you, to make you whole. Here, let me tell you how. And I relate to you all the trouble I've gone to, all my tireless efforts on your behalf, all the blows I've warded off. And what do I want in return? Why, nothing but your love. Is that too much to ask? Is it? You look up at me…your face a mask…you look up at me… Don't look at me like that, I say…your face contorted and yet unable to scream…you look up at me…your mouth opening and closing, opening and closing, opening and closing…

Don't worry, I say. It's alright. There's still tomorrow. It hasn't come yet. We'll have our picnic then.

Won't we, my salvationed one?

ASGARD'S LIGHT

1. Notes to an Anonymous Friend:

You will help me, yes? Don't make me plead. I despise pleading. More than anything I despise pleading. You're the only one who will help me. You must. I've called you my friend and that might be wishful thinking. But I'm certain that, if you're not my friend, at least we don't know each other well enough for you to be my ill-wisher. Or, God forbid, my outright enemy, come down from the lamprey rainbow with magic sword in hand to cut me to shreds. Don't you agree? I'm sure you do. Otherwise, you wouldn't have bothered to read this far. Otherwise, you would already have torn these notes to shreds and tossed them contemptuously in the fire-place – not even bothering to read to the point where I describe precisely those actions, so predictable yet still so heart-rending and true to life.

To tell the truth, I know more about you than I've let on. Let's see if I get this right. You're a little longer in the tooth, a little less hairy, a little more shrunken, a little further from in-between things. Yes? How's that so far? Your face has been described as dramatic, that of a religious fanatic and repulsively attractive in its own dark way. You've been labelled a pessimist, a contemporary absurdist, a debunker of human feeling, a shallow involuted person and a creature atrophied by profound indifference to the world around him. Correct? You've no answer for these charges and, in fact, are slightly flattered by them and the righteous tone in which they're delivered. You get along poorly indeed with your "fellow creatures." This arises from the consideration that you are superior to them because of your wit, natural aptitude for learning, creative abilities and innate sensitivities. Yes? Or is it that you don't consider yourself human at all: at times, supra- and at others, sub-? Aha, touched a nerve there, didn't I?

You've been forced into accepting a menial, unrewarding position, a position not at all in keeping with your education and potential social status, until such time as your particular worth is recognized. No, scratch that. That's utterly wrong. Like me, you're more than satisfied with the task of prime machine-tender for the automatic box maker. Your duty is to oil it every hour or so, to keep its parts from seizing, to make sure its timing isn't off by more than a microsecond for every inspection period. Do you love the machine? Ah, love is such an illogical step one's always hoping to take it without having noticed taking it. You know what I mean, don't you? Besides, it could lead to a serious mangling if you're not careful. The machine, I mean. I know. By sheer coincidence, I too tend a machine – but one that does exactly the opposite job.

You constantly rail against daily routine, would neither eat nor sleep if it were possible and begrudge the toilet its share of what you engagingly call your post-essence. There's something more than slightly distasteful about you, in the manner in which you dress, talk, walk, stammer, shop. Small things frighten you; phones make you seize up; mosquitos drive you into paroxysms of slap-happy madness which you're fond of analyzing as they're taking place. The idea of suicide you've converted into your own personal domain, though you realize you'll never kill yourself. It's the thought that counts, *n'est-ce pas*?

Lastly, you have no use for physical affection of any kind, let alone sex, both "normal" or of the aberrated variety. And yet, you have been and still are involved in an intense sexual relationship with a woman of carefree tendencies who suffers from the peculiar illness of being in love with you. Yes, I know. It's the type of word best left out of a serious discussion. This woman uses it in the same way she would "bread" or "run" or "Kleenex". It is her standard curse. You don't show it but it angers you to the core: like the sight of Canada geese heading south or talk about the "natural order of things". You lash back with all your considerable and deep-cutting wit. Okay, okay. So perhaps "wit" isn't the right word. A shrugging of the shoulders when she says something (the sunset as an example *par excellence*) is beautiful; an enraptured and joyous overture to describe an object (wet dog turd?) she loathes; the refusing of the slightest intimacy when she's in heat – and vice versa, a constant pestering like a whining pet at the most inopportune times. Later, of course, there must be the "making up." Ah, the making up. And the all made up.

You possess a personal yet highly codified set of moral rules more strict than those objectively offered by the state – or by anyone else around you. That's because, while the majority tends towards mediocrity, you are extreme – in the extreme. Scruples are your main characteristic (the building of categorical imperatives) and they bracket your personality like ever-tightening braces. You are, in other words, constantly reconstructing the cell around you that others, in the mistaken belief you wish to escape, persist in tearing town. You join no movement, be it political, social or artistic; are neither conservative nor liberal (neither left of right nor right of left); can't be carried away by the infection of the crowd; and despise being held up as the mirror for someone else's actions. A case in point: At the time of the bell-bottomed jean craze, you wouldn't be caught dead wearing bell-bottom jeans for fear you'd be identified with the other bell-bottom jean wearers. The moment they fell out of fashion, however… You'll never laugh, ride bicycles, swim, enjoy yourself or, in general, forget who you are. At least, not without a generous quantity of wine. Or beer. Mead? Hard liquor? Drugs? It's a matter of taste. You prefer to be a majority of one, stranded in your corner with wet paint all around you and that snaking rainbow bridge too far for you to reach. Nothing will induce you to stamp yourself with any identification marks whatsoever. You're pleased as punch when someone says he/she has known you for a donkey's age and yet still doesn't understand you, still hasn't fathomed you. And, true amoeba, you're always ready to shift allegiance (or better still to split) the moment someone comes too close to what you think yourself to be, to that hiding place where your "true" nature is kept. These mercenary actions don't affect your moral standards in the least – they're at your core, remember – and tend rather to build up an orchestrated pattern of mystery around you.

You'll help me then because I know you so very well and yet not at all. You'll visit me and tell me what to do, how to go about freeing myself from the consequences of my actions. Why I picked *you* for this task is perhaps uppermost on your mind at this moment, isn't it? You've never involved yourself with anyone before – not even with your own relatives, with those who have a natural claim to you – so why should you involve yourself with me, right?

Well, I could say you'll help me out of self-pity. You were walking down a deserted street in the early morning, down one of countless similar if not quite parallel streets in an area of the city caught between deepening squalor and surface respectability. Returning from a night of multiple fornication perhaps? Or smoky games of chance with an ace up your sleeve? At any rate, you were suddenly confronted by the pitiable figure of a cripple (sorry, handicapped person) holding a lunch bag in his rotting claw. As *you* weren't about to get out of *his* way, he avoided you by moving into the centre of the street, wading knee-deep in crumpled cigarette papers and chocolate wrappers. His particular mode of locomotion – a shuffling of uncontrollable itches followed by a mucoid spoor – was enough to turn your stomach. You wished the bag in his hand might be a merciful bomb with which he would embrace his unwholesome – and not very potent – God. You waited patiently for the explosion, the flying bits of flesh and bone and brain, confident you could dodge the shock wave with minimal damage because you, at least, weren't crippled (sorry, differently enabled). Instead, he collapsed unceremoniously on the street, fell with a violent thud and then struggled fiercely to right himself. This proved difficult, gravity being what it is in this part of the universe. A street cleaner chugged by unconcerned, narrowly avoiding him with its armoured wheels and spraying him with a combination of mud and water. He groped, slithering, reaching for a nearby lamppost. He grovelled, suddenly grown articulate, fixing your eye with his: "Help me. Please. My mother almost miscarried me, suffering from scissored legs, squeezing my poor soft grey matter between her vice-thighs till I popped out into a light that wasn't natural, a light that was as blinding as the end of the world." Imploring, he held out his claw, but as you reflected on the sorrows and deprivations suffered by the handicapped (crippled, disabled, differently enabled) and other uncompleted, imperfect creatures, your feet carried you away. Carried you forever into the murky realm of a hopeless self-pity.

And so who will help you? An anonymous friend in turn being helped by another anonymous friend? The beauty of that system lies in eternal non-contact, in the fact a handicapped (maimed, disadvantaged) person might be helping you or you a handicapped (paralyzed, amputated) person without ever running the risk of being disgusted. Particularly appropriate for leper colonies turned into mental hospitals and old age homes. No slavery is involved. No mumbled thank you's or polite bowings of the head. How may I help you? Scrape, scrape. Ah, the whispered obsequence of a thousand department store clerks, hands held in prayer before them. How can you help me? It'll be obvious once my story unfolds. You

who are so like me and yet so utterly different…you can fail me. I rely on our shared demon to communicate what I can't.
Yes?

The story:

At the time the police brought me in for questioning, I firmly believed I was innocent. Murder? Did they mention previously the nature of the crime or did I simply jump to that conclusion, surmising my guilt from the looks on their faces? At any rate, I could prove that on the night the crime was alleged to have been committed I was in my studio painting. I remember clearly, for it was my masterpiece, my definitive statement, the oeuvre with which I would make my mark. I called it *Full Lunacy Over Valhalla*: one thousand square feet of solid blue on which was surmounted a large orange ball, darkening at the edges. You must see it. I insist. It will serve to change your life around, one of those seminal visions. My key is beneath the welcome mat. After trying to open the door with it and finding it's the wrong one, you'll simply turn the handle and go in. The painting will be there against the far wall – to catch the north light, of course, the light of Asgard, where the numb feeling of cold is all there is and all there'll ever be. And you will undoubtedly gasp at the sight of it, at the raw majesty it suggests, at the hopelessness of its vision.

I said that, at first, I was convinced absolutely of my innocence. I was, after all, a pacifist, not in the least inclined to violence. Later, I became uncertain. The police presented unshakeable evidence of my guilt – a gory dagger with my fingerprints on it and a child's pair of black patent leather shoes stained by long gashes of dried blood. This blood, as well as the drops on the dagger, proved to be that of the murdered person. It seemed like paint to me when the shoes were presented as evidence at the trial. And perhaps it was. But I was so swept away by the force of the prosecutor's impassioned argument I forgot to whisper my suspicions in the defence lawyer's ear.

The motive, they said, was envy. Speculation was that, believing the boy to be a superior painter and potential rival, I'd lured him to my studio and slit his throat – after forcing him to paint my masterpiece. That is a possibility. Who am I, child of the Teutonic Freud, to dispute the search for motive? For emotional cause and effect? In fact, I like the idea of envy. At least it points to something human.

During the pre-trial period, the police – big, brutal, crewcut men with swollen-shut eyes – were especially kind to me, even to the point of removing their uniforms in my presence and putting on robes resembling those worn by self-whipping monks. Next to the cell itself – a veritable palace with a colour television, automatic toilet that flushed every hour on the half-hour, books from Botticelli to the Bible, the latest in fine arts and pornographic magazines, a soft bed and a wide variety of exotic food – their kindness and attentiveness worried me the most. It had a simpering, paternal touch to it, a pat on the head, a tweak of the downy cheek, a gentle whispered word for the little infant in me. The thought of my guilt redoubled. After all, why should they take so much trouble with me if I were innocent? There was no point to that. Who wants an innocent man? Were they capable of "I think that you think that I think" machinations? And, if they were, where did it stop? Where did it all end?

My parents came to see me without showing the least surprise or interest in my incarceration. My mother – I believe she called me some name or other but I can't remember – commented briefly on the pleasant surroundings and the need for fresh flowers. I felt as a man should when visited in jail for the first time by relatives or close friends. I honestly wished to kill them both. This confirmed my guilt. They remained for the longest time, taking turns in their assaults. While one talked, or wept, the other inspected the cell or stared at me. Then, by subtle shifts, they would change positions.

On hearing the toilet flush, my father rushed in, dropping his pants along the way. Apparently, he'd been through this before (a brother perhaps, explaining the link to my own genetic criminality?). My mother, growing older by the moment as if on cue, urged me to confess. I couldn't stand the thought of her hair turning any whiter so I told her all she wanted to know: Yes, yes, yes. I had done it. I had done it all. She smiled like any mother would. Then, in one quick motion, she pulled a derringer dangling from a string between her legs and pointed it at my heart. She said she loved me too much to allow someone else to kill me. So she'd do it herself. I fell to my knees in appreciation. The gun clicked. My father returned, a disappointed look on his face. I'm sorry, he said, zipping up. I guess you'll have to live with it till the next flush.

Afterthought: Did my girlfriend visit me during the night wearing a bathing suit and carrying a little boy on her shoulders? Or was it all part of the same nightmare?

The trial, of course, turned out to be a mere formality. What was the point when I knew I was guilty and that justice could only be served with my removal? When I told the court as much, the judge (a kindly white-haired woman wielding an immense yet familiar hammer that sparked when she banged it) smiled and said guilt was not something for me to determine but rather a matter for the jury to decide. I remained silent for the rest of the trial, refusing to answer even questions put to me by my own attorney. In the end, much to my dismay, despite my screams and remonstrations, they reduced the charge due to a technicality. Instead of first-degree murder, they found me guilty of having killed myself at the moment I both realized and renounced my talent. And sentenced me to this life ever after without the possibility of even a single single reprieve, a single death along the way.

The notes continued:

You don't believe me, do you? Well, I don't blame you. I don't believe myself. I've never painted in my life. Nor have I ever been in jail. My parents, God bless their peasant souls, tend gardens, make beds and practice the art of flipping *fritatta*. You're absolutely right not to believe me. I was just practising. After all, my duty is the telling of fictions. It's safer: truth is the worm in the meat. I tell lies to avoid the Big Lie. You understand that, don't you? Don't you? My friend? How could I possibly tell the truth? Pick it out of the dense flea-bitten air with a black glove? Chop away the chaos to find the germ of order within? Nail it down to the corpse of what is really real – until that too explodes into just one more mockery of ice and snow?

Here is what I remember – or care to: She was a fine swimmer, an excellent swimmer, a lovely swimmer, almost a wonderful swimmer. Fine, excellent, lovely, wonderful. All meaningless but fun to roll around the tongue, full of the possibility of warmth and the illusion of sense. Let's put it this way: she swam while I couldn't even wade, couldn't even keep myself afloat. But one must make the most of one's handicaps (encripplements, maimings, disadvantages). So it's clear the inability to wade should be a fabulist's first attribute. The second is the inability to get drunk. To be drunk is to be human. Am I not right? Inability must rule. Only room for one skill.

Both she and I loathed beaches, especially the crowded north-ern inland ones (most of them now closed or turned into experi-mental labs for toxic materials) that smelled more like cheese than ocean spray. Fetid, dimly lit lagoons left behind when the ice retreated (temporarily, I'm told). However, while I sat on the sand churning my loathing into a hatred with no outlet, she, armed with a constant smile, would swim out past the reaches of human emo-tion. Or so I believed. And, lest you forget, this *is* the story of my beliefs. I envied her those moments wrapped in primary substance – and plankton-like creatures not yet injected with deadly viruses. But there was always the consolation that if she stopped moving for even one second, if she lacked alertness for the blink of an eye, she would quickly touch the edge of something hard and sharp. Quite a consolation, don't you think?

In the summer, every chance we got, every moment we were free from work and the sun was shining, the breeze warm, she insisted on being near water – even if that meant busing it tens, nay hundreds, of kilometres. She said that children love water so much because they are of it. Intimate. Not yet separated from the elemental source, the sac that held their essence. And she wished to be near water because children were her main preoccupation. What childlike fancies did she perceive in me? I followed her sul-lenly, sitting crablike on the desultory beaches, on the yellowing cement of abandoned piers and crumbling breakwaters. I became quite adept at building sand castles which she'd destroy as soon as she returned from her sojourns. Not maliciously, but with a casual stroke of her milk-white, wrinkled foot. And she laughed at me for always being the only one who didn't take off his clothes, who didn't come equipped with a set of mandatory bathing trunks. "You're such a bore." Gleaming smile. "Bores bore me." There were times when I could play along with her – "If I take these clothes off, I'll disappear. Poof!" But mostly I acted hurt and she turned away for another swim muttering in disbelief. Or went off to play with the usual squad of children that waited patiently for her just beyond my reach. Funny how the squad was never quite the same yet always banded together, spreading their tentacles like some giant octopus that had strayed too close to shore. She wedged her way into the centre by some means I never discovered nor believe I would understand even if it were shown to me. It was as if she could turn two-dimensional for the time it took to penetrate their midst. Naturally, they wanted nothing to do with me, would go out of their way to avoid me. I reciprocated. Sometimes, I felt they were turning her away from me as well. Children are insidious. By that I mean simply that they're inside everything. I could only look on. It's frustrating to only look on and not even to enjoy the scientist's pleasure of experimenting. Ah, the sweet taste of dissection, the lingering feel of the scalpel cutting, penetrating, the…sigh…

On the beach, I spent my time reading whatever technical manuals and instructional material I could lay my hands on. This usually consisted of out-of-date *Popular Mechanics* and *Hi-Tech Electronics* magazines. It protected me somewhat from the others and from the perpetual wind. But, no matter how careful I was, my mouth would eventually fill with sand and I'd end up chewing on large quantities, unable to spit it all out. This was inevitable, one of the dangers of frequenting beaches. At first, I found the whole process extremely distasteful and it made it difficult to hold down any food I'd eaten beforehand. Then it became a take it or leave it proposition, an undeclared truce between flesh and sand. Finally, towards the end, I took positive joy in filling my mouth with handfuls of sand and chewing. In fact, it was hard to read about the smooth-meshing gears and perpetual motion machines without a mouthful of grit to give them substance. For the longest time after I'd stopped going to beaches, or during the endless winter days when the light barely climbed over the horizon, I could still feel those grains of sand. As if out of nowhere, the urge to chew would come on – at home as I readied for bed, at work as I fitted more boxes into the machine, on the street between bus transfers. And my teeth would grate together; the perpetual-motion wheels would turn; the hairs would rise along my spine.

It was particularly strong in the morning, that point when wakefulness is perfectly balanced and the sun would come peeking through the bedroom window with its cute message: "Arise, oh pale, flesh-bound one. Your perfect machine awaits you." My machine? But yes. No point denying it. It *was* my machine, wasn't it? I've long since abandoned the pretense of disassociation – just as I assume you have. Where would we be without our personal machine? Even today, I feel its magnetic pull (something to do with the electrical configuration, no doubt). It carried out – and, I presume, still does carry out – its rudimentary, fundamental task effortlessly, squeezing the old over-used and thus useless boxes into the least possible space, gift-wrapping them with metal straps and depositing them at the other end in neat cubes. How it did this I never bothered finding out. Does one probe the mechanics, the inner workings, the guts of a perfect lover? Those who tended to the machine's internal needs knew it infinitely better than I. Those who had built it were even more familiar with its parts. But, despite that, it was *my* machine and had been *my* machine for all save the first few months when I was apprenticing at the shop. Those early days were frigid with timidity and shyness on both our parts. We were feeling each other out, looking for a way to get acquainted. Sometimes it would sputter and groan as I approached still not fully awake from fitful sleep; or it would suddenly disgorge a mashed-up box left in its bowels from the previous day, plopping it at my feet like a tender offering. It seemed we would go on this way, unable to take that final step that marks true intimacy, for the rest of our time together: always the novice; never to have mastered or been mastered. But then one morning the machine started up by itself, took the initiative as it were, as one of the workers stuffed some torn cartons into it. He lost his arm, sliced off cleanly at the shoulder by the recently honed blades. It really was quite interesting with the worker standing there transfixed, neither screaming nor fainting, simply watching as the blood pumped out of his stump. Later that night, after an ambulance had taken the unfortunate fellow away, the other workers turned nasty and violent. They began to curse the machine, tried to sabotage it, called down the powers of heaven on it (what exactly is God's position on recalcitrant machines? Creations not directly his/her own?). Until, at last, the foreman, even though sympathetic to their cause, had to drive them away purely for economic reasons. On the other hand, I found this the signal I'd been waiting for. I patted the machine gently, whispered sweet nothings to it, lubricated whatever joints I could find. After all, I had no reason to doubt that I'd be working next to it for the rest of my life. Striking up an understanding was imperative. Best of all, there was minimal loss of production. Only one package had to be discarded – and that for obvious reasons. Through it all, what struck me was the professional attitude and disposition of my machine. Heckled, spat upon and monkeyed with (spanners can be deadly), it continued on its majestic course, producing one set of perfectly-packaged boxes after another, until I was ordered to stop it. No one else dared come near and they grumbled instead that the machine should be destroyed, put down like a pet that has suddenly turned vicious. I really can't understand how some people think. It had done nothing, was guilty of no crime. At worst, the switch had slipped or it hadn't been oiled properly or a gear had seized. But what had that to do with the machine? Perhaps they were envious? Do you think so? Do you think that might explain it? It wouldn't be the first time.

The undated diary:

A. A flock of birds buried itself in the sand today. They moved in unison and in a barely visible blur, as if one organism controlled them. Birds never get sand in their eyes and mouths. I wonder what the reason for this is. Just another useless question. After a few moments of immobility beneath the sand, they burst out into the sky – like an arrow piercing to the very heart of it.

She ignores me more and more. Not for some other man. Or woman. She ignores us all, the beached creatures drying in the sand, walking through us whenever she gets the opportunity. Only the children she hugs and kisses. And then into the water. I tried practising all day being a child – the thumb-sucking mixed with a spiteful precociousness – but I couldn't stick at it because it's too hard. Much too hard. I don't know how children do it really.

B. One of her favourites has lost his ears. That's her expression. I laughed when she told me his parents were dissatisfied with his ears and so had then altered through surgery. She cried and refused to go swimming. How silly! Don't you agree? She lay down beside me, the tears brimming over and spilling down the side of her face before being lost forever in the thirsty, leechlike earth. Then she suddenly stood up and rushed to caress him. I tried to read, stuffing more and more sand into my mouth. Tonight, she turned her back when I reached for her, saying it was inappropriate as she was in mourning. Is the loss of your ears or a part of them really so horrible? She suggests I cut off my ears to see how it feels. I remind her it was a question of aesthetics not torture. This changes nothing in her opinion. I have to agree: aesthetics can be torture and vice versa.

C. Overjoyed today by the fact I am not the only one on the beach who doesn't remove his clothes. Overjoyed. He's a moderately old man (his description) with no teeth and protruding cheekbones who calls himself Mr. Loki. Or Low-key. He blocks out the sun, a hunchbacked shadow, and tells me suddenly he's been observing me for weeks. You always start castles of gigantic size and complexity, he says, and end up with one-room huts whose walls are a metre thick. Why? Funny I haven't noticed him before. He's as conspicuous as a black spot in the sun: an ancient coat down to his ankles, a misshapen, grease-lined pork-pie hat tilted across one eye, thick old orange-coloured work shoes over crusted wool socks. He asked me if the sand was good. I didn't answer. He said it was all right for me not to answer, him being a stranger and all. That should be a general principle – not answering, that is – as you never know when even the closest of friends will turn into strangers. "At the drop of a hat," he said, demonstrating by dropping his own and then whirling it back onto his head before it hit the ground.

He said that in his youth – a sigh that seemed to signify eons – he too sat constantly on beaches, cursing the air and the people. But since then he had mellowed, had accepted the gravity of the situation. Now, he paints. I was startled. An artist of the old school, I said to myself. No government subsidies or grants. No attempts at ingratiating himself with the reigning bureaucracy. Or orthodoxy. He offered to show me some of his work. I was delighted. Overjoyed – startled – delighted—

For a blessed afternoon I forgot completely about her. The last time I looked, she was swimming in gigantic circles around the lake, starting from the outer edges and working towards the centre. Someone was pointing at her. There was something wrong with the shape of his head. Come, Mr. Loki said, helping me up. His hand was smooth as he gripped mine, that of a much younger man. I followed along. It was the first time I'd actually seen the town behind the beach. Mr. Loki led me down the dusty streets, stopping occasionally to talk to other old people who sat on their front porches or puttered about in their gardens, gardens gleaming with unnaturally vivid colours. Only the old ones are left, he said. They have no place better to go. So, they come here – to the edge of nowhere. Everyone else is gone. No patience, no stamina. Ah, here we are! My masterpiece. I looked around. Masterpiece? He pointed to a building at the end of the road. It was a bright red schoolhouse with a glossy green roof that dazzled in the sun. I turned, ready to spit out that no one made a fool of me, that I wasn't a yokel whose idea of art stopped at country fair baskets. But then I noticed he was totally earnest. It's never been used, he said. The ultimate symbol of birth control. We went closer. He talked about the time he'd put into this building, getting it ready, painting with painstaking care every little cornice, every shutter and windowsill. As he talked, completely immersed in his recital, I went around the back. Shit! Was nothing sacred? Someone had defaced his work with obscene scribblings and what looked like the image of a boy with an enormous penis masturbating beneath the slivered moon. I came around the front again, hoping to distract him so he wouldn't go to the back and notice the defacement. But there was no need. The old man was caught in a reverie, remembering the days when his artistry was at its peak and making gummy smacking sounds with his lips.

D. We've just returned from the beach – at night. As horrible and long a night as I've ever experienced. Another of her bright ideas. Oh, it sounded so romantic: a warm close embrace as we knelt in the sand, tongue to tongue, legs rubbing, the squeak of bathing suits, a hazy moonlight sanctifying our spontaneous coupling. Do humans really do that? Roll in the hay? Jump on the wagon? Beat in the back seat?

At least, I said to myself, there won't be anyone around to distract her, especially no children tugging at her arms, begging her to play with them or fix their booboos. But it made little difference.

Perhaps the fault lies with me. Perhaps I should learn to swim. A child can do it, why can't you? After trying to coax me in vain into the water with a promise she wouldn't let me sink, she leapt up in a fury and threw herself at the nearest wave, uttering words I won't repeat. "You'll hurt yourself on a rock," I whispered. "One of these days, you'll do yourself damage." But I didn't follow her in. I felt I'd made enough concessions just removing my clothes. I did regret, however, not having brought a flashlight. For it was much too dark to read, especially the fine print on the patent applications and instruction manuals.

When she re-emerged from the water, she announced that she was no longer angry at me and that we should do this more often. Her wet body stank horribly, as if someone had just pried open a rotten clam. Casually, she took off her bathing suit and lay down beside me, flicking water into my face. Come on, she said, massaging her breasts. I concentrated on the thick, one-roomed castle before me. She stood up, pulling me up with her. I waited a few moments, then sat down again. What is one supposed to do? Follow? Images of a daytime beach where a long line of children weaves behind her like a multicoloured anaconda. Only poisonous. Infinitely more poisonous. She sighed and dressed. You're hopeless, she said. Let's go. The finishing touch was our stumbling into another couple further down the beach in the final throes of sexual collusion, their bellies slapping wetly, backs arched at impossible angles, the suck-a-suck of wet sand helping to drown their rabid cries. They didn't even stop to let us by, even though we practically stepped over them. I glanced back in awe; she with what I imagined was envy.

E. Mr. Loki asked me today if I liked children. I was about to answer when he told me not to bother. Answers, he said, are always lies. I puzzled over that for a while and decided he was right. I would have lied. Then he asked if I believed in children per se or were they merely perennial dwarfs and midgets who created each other through some alchemy of innocence while the rest of us were born adults – already guilty and useless? I pointed to the girl circling in the water and smiled. He understood. I told him he didn't really understand. You're right, he said. Beneath the understanding there's always another layer. No, I said, there really was nothing to understand. There were no layers. Just a thick surface coating that penetrated deeper and deeper into things till they vanished.

You're neurotic, he said. I'm not neurotic. The things I'm not afraid of, I despise. He asked what I liked. I said I liked neurotics. But only the kind met in books. A real live neurotic muttering and crawling along chipped walls and cobblestone streets would only unnerve me, would make me incapable of action. As, for that matter, do normal people. Well then, he said, making his point like a lawyer, what kind of a relationship do you have with that girl? Another smile. Relationship? Perhaps a barely tolerable one. Or was it that I wished no one else to have her? Balanced on a dull knife-edge that faked emotion on both sides. With my machine? Splendid. Couldn't be better. It never failed, never said no, never booked off sick, never made me have ugly feelings, never laughed. Never decided it was time for a swim. Seems a bit silly, doesn't it? A machine satisfying a human being? Mr. Loki didn't answer, simply picking up a fistful of sand and throwing it into the air.

F.   It happened. We had an argument. More precisely, she had an argument. She told me she was sick and tired of swallowing my moral disapproval for something as innocent and harmless as leading 10-year-olds by the hand. There was no satisfying me. And, furthermore, she could no longer take my silence as she swam out. I was a cold brutal non-entity with a scar for a soul. There was no denying she was right. Perhaps simply a cold brutal non-entity as I didn't believe in souls. An apology was in order.

That I didn't offer one was simply a reflection of the enjoyment I got from listening to her. She ripped the magazine from my hands and hurled it into the sand. When that didn't satisfy her, she started to tear it apart page by page. Specifications for perpetual motion machines floated on the scummy sea. Finally, when that got no reaction (I was still too fascinated), she swore and threw herself into the water.

Mr. Loki, standing behind me the whole time, said girls really don't understand the printed page. They read books but don't fully accept them – even though they'd soon be the last repository of literacy in the world. I was in no mood for a philosophic discussion. He talked to himself for a few minutes more and then fell silent. The beach smelled of oil, cheese, soggy paper, monstrous inventions—

What could I do but melt under that sun? Construct an image? Yes, get to constructing then. The crowd moved like a wasp nest towards the commotion in the water. The lifeguard was dragging something towards the shore – a sack, a piece of driftwood, a body. Someone shouted that a child had almost drowned, had been saved at the last moment by a young lady. I knew in my heart who that "young lady" was. Errands of mercy! Let the little bas— boys drown!

A few hands in the crowd pointed in my direction and then everyone turned to look at me. The people parted. I saw her at that moment lying on the beach. It had been the other way around. She was the one who almost drowned. Saved by her short-eared child-lover? Not true! A blatant untruth! I saw myself rising in a blur of anguish, smile on my face, reaching down to drown him, to take him by those pathetic quasi-ears and slowly lower his deformed head into the water, feeling him thrash beneath me like an animal about to be slaughtered. Oh, the exquisite joy, the raw naked flash of power searing through my flesh. The thought quickly passed. I hadn't the courage. I could as much drown him as save her. There was no point in helping. Or even thinking about it. She would simply have fallen down again smack in the middle of the street. I mean, water.

Mr. Loki tapped me on the shoulder and pointed. She lay on the beach, her bathing cap removed, a strand of hair across her mouth. The lifeguard brushed the hair aside and, pinching her nostrils, brought his mouth over hers. Several of the bystanders, seeing I wouldn't approach, came towards me instead. As soon as I realized their intention, I stood up and walked off in the other direction. They yelled at me, but I knew them not. I was a stranger to the beach. Mr. Loki followed me, cackling insanely, throwing his hat high into the air and allowing it to sink back onto his head. Fool. Why don't you rush over to her, gasp out your tender emotions, ask worried questions about her health, clasp her sweet face between your hands, implore the Lord that he might spare her, promise Him anything for her life, promise to marry her after her first gasping breath? No, instead I found myself up against the front door of the little red schoolhouse, the empty little red schoolhouse, the never-occupied little red schoolhouse. My trousers were at my feet. Mr. Loki was kneeling down before me. Or it may have been the other way around.

What I remember:

What I remember: No, enclosed in this pale, lightless room since that day, I've never seen her again. Mr. Loki waited outside the door for a while, telling me stories about deserted cities and their slow reversion to jungle, the vines pushing up through the concrete. Here, let me relate one of them for you: "Rigg was a vegetarian of the first order. He would eat nothing that had anything to do with meat. When he was young, his parents attributed this to a passing fancy he'd outgrow at puberty. To prepare him, they made it a point to mix chunks of meat into the cereal gruel he preferred. Unbeknown to them, he never ate these mixtures, sniffing them out carefully and then slipping them to the ragged, bellows-chested dogs that wandered about the camp. Puberty came and went. During the initiation rites, Rigg was pinned to the earth while raw meat was forced down his throat. He almost choked on his vomit, spewing the pieces high into the air. The rest of the initiates moved away. This re-enforced his decision to scorn whatever society offered. He avoided the opportunity to take part in the cyclic battles with neighbours; he turned down intimations and invitations of love (from both sexes); he shunned the political processes. The danger of such choices is obvious. Rigg's community was built on a basis of tolerance and goodwill, much more so than any modern society. However, there are limits. Already, many took the opportunity to spit on him as they passed. And even his parents were losing their natural affection for him. After all, what would happen when they died? How would he be able to carry out his filial obligations, the obligations that allowed them to pass into the spirit world? The rubber band describing the relation between Rigg and his society stretched to its breaking point and snapped the day the village was attacked by a group of barbaric pale-faced marauders who raped and pillaged while Rigg sat there, idiotic grin on his face, contemplating the problems of perspective and depth of field. As his mother lay on the ground, recovering her strength from the combined assaults of a dozen or so warriors, his father came up quietly behind him and, with one clean blow, lopped off his head. The next day, the whole village – or what remained of it – celebrated, feasting on some of the best meat ever – tender, juicy and unspoiled by the previous consumption of flesh."

That was several days ago. I've heard nothing from the old man since. Tell me another, Mr. Loki, I said. I like your stories. No answer. Okay, then. Okay. Just go take a look behind your red schoolhouse, your precious schoolhouse. Go on. There's a little surprise for you. Still no response. Perhaps he, too, has abandoned me.

Yesterday, a letter was slipped under my door. Even though unsigned, I assume it was from her. It was filled with 'Ahs' and 'Ohs' and 'I regrets.' Even little drops that resembled tears but probably were judicious sprinklings of perfumed water. The P.S. informed me that this person had made the decision of a lifetime: "Oh, farewell. I've spent too much time thinking only of myself. Now, I'm off to help save the swollen-bellied children of the Third World." Indeed.

I presume my machine is lost as well. Someone else – a one-armed man perhaps – has taken my place, stroking it under that one swaying light bulb, oiling its essential parts, making sure it performs up to its exacting standards. Or perhaps simply abusing it. In any case, I've lost it forever. All because of a human being. And those insidious little creatures with life and hope and the ability to swim. But calmness is all. In any case, who wants to swim out? Only a madman.

You'll help me:

You'll help me. Yes? Take time off from your own machine-tending to pay me a visit? I'm waiting at this moment for you. The knife is outside my door. It's the long thin one in case there are others – necessarily false ones which may have been placed there to confuse you. I must warn you, however, that I'll be ready for you. I'll have an identical blade on me. But you can still surprise me. Sure, you can. How? you ask. Well, why not…yes, why not disguise yourself? Disguises are fun – and practical, too. But, quick now, as what? There are so many things, an infinite number of things, one could become with the proper attitude and attire. As a…as a…as a writer? Too obvious. Too symbolic. A killer, then? No, no. Too stylized and impractical. Why would I let a killer freely into the room? Of course, of course. I have it now! You, my anonymous friend, my fellow machine-tender, you must pin back your ears, slick your hair, throw out your cynicism and…and…and…disguise yourself…as a…as a…as a child!

That'll do.

Yes, in this dim place of disappearances and dark-hued rainbows, of lunar lakes and velvet machinery, of a light that never reaches me, that'll most certainly do.

BANDAGES

Maybe it's only your imagination – it *has* been acting up of late – but it seems that more and more people on the street are sporting bandages. Some have very tiny ones, more like patches really or see-through Band-Aids; others are covered in great big swaths, wound round and round their arms. Or their chests. Or their heads.

The first thing you do is to look around for signs of war. War, you know from past experience and TV/Internet/YouTube footage, has the tendency to cause a flowery blossoming of bandages, a veritable explosion, many with untidy splotches of blood threatening to seep through. But, though news of invasions, suicide bombings, genocide, and wholesale death and destruction fills the international airwaves, all the wars and mass killing are a long distance off – at least for the time being. In your immediate vicinity, in the local post-yuppie neighbourhood that you patrol, peace and sunshine, love and conventional snobbery prevail. Oh sure, there are the occasional gangland slaying attempts, baseball bat attacks by jealous wives/lovers and, once in a long while, a shoot-'em-up armed robbery. But that wouldn't be enough to account for the proliferation of bandages on the street. They even start showing up at the chic terraces and swank cafés where the customers sit posing like wax statues that would most definitely melt under direct light – or, at least, direct questioning.

"Bandage? What bandage?" the slinky woman at the table next to yours says when you finally get up the nerve to hint at her mode of dress. For a moment she looks about in alarm, fluttering her long-lashed eyelids, then laughs and goes back to sipping her cinnamon decaf *frappo cappo*.

"Oh, you mean this" – pointing to the peach-coloured gauze wrapped loosely around her head. "I like the style, you know. It's in, the hurt look. Kinda vulnerable and innocent. The Japanese invented it, I think. Or maybe I saw it on a runway in Milan. Yes, that's it. The Rumble in Rwanda Night on the Town. All the models wore this marvellous refugee clothing."

"No, darling," the equally slinky man across from her chimes in. "It was that guy Khadaffi. Remember? After the Americans bombed him? Or Saddam? No, no. Now I remember. Bin Laden."

So, that's it. Like everything else, it's merely a matter of fashion and taste, of élan and style, perhaps tied in with the notion that it isn't too healthy to appear too healthy these days. What with strapping young fellows just itching to send messages of explosive impact.

Or is that it, really?

"Fashion!" the old man on the park bench bellows when it's suggested he is right in style – *à la mode* – with the large filthy bandage he has wrapped around his left arm. "What's it bloody well got to do with fashion? Do you think I enjoy walking around with this pus-spewing wound that won't heal? And for which the doctors can do not a bloody thing? Except to say it's the result of growing old, a result of long-ago torture, a result of watching my wife being raped by half-a-dozen animals pretending to be soldiers. Eh, young man? Answer me that. Do you think it's fashionable to have to change the dressing twice daily, to have to turn my face away from my own flesh and blood? Here, you wanna see it? You wanna see this fashion, as you call it? Here, have a look."

And, all the while, under the green shade and the peaceful twittering of birds and children, the old man is busy unravelling his increasingly caked covering. With every layer the old man takes off, the bloody yellowish spot becomes more noticeable, larger in size, more frightening. You sense it is time to move away, to back out of the park – before you too are thrown into his nightmarish world.

"I'll show you fashion," the old man screams as he suddenly tears after you, the bandage flapping in the wind like a bird of prey. "Stop! Stop that man! I want to show him something. He won't let me show it to him. Stop! He's shirking his responsibilities! I want him to be my witness. I want the world to remember."

You escape into an alley, all out of breath, hiding behind a huge pile of rubbish, some of it – judging by the scent and consistency – from the hospital across the way. From there, you see the old man rush by, now waving a completely bandage-free arm. Arm, did I say? More like a gnarled branch than a human limb.

So, it isn't all fashion. There are actually some people out there who are hurt, wounded, not whole. Victims. Of war? Torture? Personal vendettas? Ancient family feuds? Runaway tractor trailers? And they wear the bandages to keep the hurt from spreading, from tumbling out into the street and just lying there. Or maybe flopping about obscenely at the end of some jagged flesh.

And you learn to tell the fashionables from the truly hurt. Not that it's always easy, mind you. A person could go from fashionable to hurt in a matter of seconds, so that a chiffon headdressing for the avant-garde gallery opening might quickly turn into a life-saving tourniquet when the homemade bomb explodes (dissident, scorned, misunderstood, minimalist, gallery-lacking artists being especially ferocious).

Of course, the reverse isn't as likely but there are cases of the genuinely ill or injured disguising their hurt with fashion accessories. Or continuing to wear the bandages long after the hurting is over. Anything to keep the attention they've so painfully earned. Or not to draw the attention of those strapping young men in their buttoned-up ski jackets.

And once the strangeness of all-wrapped-up people wears off, you begin to think less and less of it till it becomes routine to see the streets filled with partial mummies. Oh, you still suffer from the occasional startle, such as the time an acrobat falls from a tree, tan-coloured bandages around both legs and chest, and exclaims: "I'm telling you it's the atmosphere; it's the acid rain. It drops on you out of the sky and where it strikes you it sizzles and burns and eats away the flesh." But, despite being dated by the use of "acid rain" rather than "climate change," that's to be expected.

As is the lecture on "How to Cover Your Psychic Scars" by a self-styled "Post-Doctoral Professor of Neurocognitive Linguistics." It turns out to be the same old thing really with the healing and bandage metaphors writ large across the blackboard and a soft-spoken man in a bald wig explaining how the modern world could not possibly save itself as it is bleeding internally. Bleeding from a huge gash few even notice. And how the wrappings are only stop-gap measures, perhaps not even covering the right wounds, etc., etc.

You walk out halfway when the post-doctoral professor launches into his demonstration of how to spot – and heal – the hurt centres through the use of an apparatus he has just recently patented. An apparatus that "analyzes the spoken word, breaks down its artificial constructs and then converts it into a deep-probing bio-logo-tool". For a nominal fee, of course.

The closest you come to recovering your old excitement is when you spot a notice on the bulletin board of your favourite espresso bar. It announces a spectacle to be held at the nearby park the following Sunday. Nothing unusual about that, you say. Sunday shows are a regular occurrence in the summer, using as a stage an octagonal bandstand that had once reverberated with old-time live music concerts before the invention of cell phones and iPods. But what attracts you is the grainy graphic on the announcement: a half-dozen or so members of a troupe wrapped completely in white bandages from head to toe – not even allowing holes for eyes or breathing space for mouths.

So intent are you on not missing this performance that you sleep on a park bench that night, covered in advertising flyers and curled up like a child against the damp. It is thus that you see, as the sun rises, the actors – seven in all – hold hands and grope to form a circle around one of the old-growth maples. Then, after breaking the circle and walking in a stumbling fashion the circumference of the park – during which they pick up several more spectators (including the old man who is still looking incredulously at his twiggy arm), they lead each other on to the old bandstand platform. And re-form their blind circle, now spread at arm's length.

In the silence that follows, or perhaps it is only your concentration that shuts everything else out as you strain to see, to understand, they slowly unravel each other's bandages. Gently unwind the strips of white gauze, inch by inch, around and around, and lower them floating to the ground.

And the first to go are their feet. And then their legs and torsos vanish. And this is followed by their arms. And their heads. And finally, their fingers, their plucking nimble fingers.

And the only things left on that platform are seven mounds of cloth, light as the feathers of invisible birds.

But, of course, that's all there is in the first place.

THE ANARCHISTS

"And so he tried to make the world
safe for when he, too, would be
helpless." —An epitaph

Lying in bed and unable to sleep anyway, Becker found it enlightening to pull the covers over his head and listen to the short-wave radio. He liked to spin the tuning dial at random, picking up far-flung signals, gravelly, even-handed, often unintelligible voices, and crackling hints of insurrections, followed inevitably by the *snap-snap* of gunfire. On this particular moon-bleached night, a Mass – being celebrated in St. Peter's where it was actually dawn – was cut off briefly by a news bulletin. "We interrupt this blessed celebration," the soothing voice intoned, "to bring you an announcement of local interest, of strictly local interest. Earlier this evening, in two widely separated sections of the city, a handicapped vendor was murdered and a bronze statue decapitated. Police are unable to say at the moment whether these two crimes took place simultaneously or simply in rapid succession." The voice faded. Becker turned up the volume and listened more closely – but that was all for the time being, save for an announcement that further details would come with the early-morning newscast. There was the sound of snoring from the adjacent bedroom – and a snuffling, braying noise like that of a contented animal removing its snout from the trough before being led off to slaughter. Becker lowered the volume again so that he had to place his ear against the speaker of the radio to better hear what was being said. The High Mass resumed at the *Introibo* (the miracle of modern technology) and continued unhindered to the end.

The police, it was whispered on the regular news hour, hadn't a clue to either crime. And it didn't even cross their minds that the murder and statue decapitation might have been the work of one and the same criminal. It never would. But, from the moment Becker first heard the report, the identity of that person was crystal clear to him. He lay back on the bed and shut his eyes, letting the warm feeling spread over him. After all, how often does one get the opportunity to savour such knowledge, to be so positive about something? Becker asked himself. Think of it: For the moment, I alone know who the criminal is. I alone. Well, except for the culprit himself – if, that is, he thought of himself as a criminal at all.

Someone was up and making noise in the kitchen. That had to be his stepfather, who in politically correct 21st-century style always arose to prepare breakfast. Becker slipped both his head and the portable radio under a pillow. It droned on, amid the static, the loss of clarity that morning brought, giving details. The handicapped vendor had been a Vietnam War amputee who pedalled a special bike with his hands because his legs had been blown away in a minefield. Death had been by garroting as he wheeled towards the corner where he waited daily with a tin cup in one hand and crumbly pencils in the other, trying to catch the eye of passersby. The murder weapon, a thin copper wire, was found neatly folded in his camouflage jacket pocket. No fingerprints could be made out. Such murders were common enough in that section of the city so as to attract little attention from the authorities. The other crime was considered both more important and more bizarre. A statue – not any statue, mind you, but of an illustrious founding father of the city – had lost its bronze head to a stick of dynamite. This dynamite, carefully measured so that it would cause damage only to a particular area, had been wrapped about the statue's neck and equipped with a thirty-minute timer. That's what made it possible for him to commit both crimes at what seemed the same time. Becker was positive. As usual, there were no witnesses to either crime and experts had already been sent to take measurements of a replacement for the statue's head. As for the amputee, well…attempts were being made to inform the next of kin – and a collection was taken up for a proper burial. Becker made a note of the address so he could consider sending his contribution. The radio announced that, on the following night, the Mass would come from the beleaguered but ever faithful Catholic minority in Beirut who, despite almost constant harassment and shifting military allegiances, risked their lives daily for the body and blood of Christ.

Becker's Notebook I:

As children, he and I had been neighbours and the closest of companions. We had revealed intimate secrets to each other because we believed secrets were the only true bonds of friendship. He told me once his worst fear was that the statues would suddenly come alive. Then, there would be no stopping them, especially those in armour and wielding swords. And the streets would reverberate with the cracking of eggshell skulls, the impaling of helpless, wriggling humans. I remember being profoundly jealous of these fears, my own being so much more petty, so much more mundane.

"Statues," he'd said to me again and again, "have fooled us into believing that they are immobile and have no life. Not true! Not true at all. They just exist in another dimension, that's all; just move too slowly for our eyes to follow. All our accidents are caused by statues; all our mistakes can be blamed on them. And cripples are dangerous,

too, because, being partially immobile and often missing parts, we pity them and think they're harmless. Wait and see. You just wait and see. It's their immobile and missing parts that'll get us, that'll do us in in the end. You wait and see."

The two parted suddenly and dramatically one night after his friend totally demolished Hephaestus, the Greek god Becker's parents kept in the backyard as a bird bath. He splintered it with a sledgehammer, pulverizing it till only the ragged-edged stand remained. Becker helped him but with none of his passion or brilliance. The last he'd heard, his friend had found himself a room in the downtown area. It was across the street from a park in which stood one of the largest, most imposing statues in the city. Becker's parents had puzzled for days over who could have committed such a senseless act of vandalism, then replaced the Hephaestus with Cronos. Becker could see his hoary face each morning as he performed his customary 100 push-ups on the bed – to the background of a call for prayer from Mecca.

There were now two people making noise in the kitchen – lovey-dovey sounds from what Becker could gather – and eggs sputtered as they fried. He clenched his fists and kicked against the mattress. How dare they? He hissed "Enough! Silence!" through his teeth. Instead, the noise increased: taps started to flow; the toilet flushed; there was the happy chirping of birds as they plucked dewy earthworms out of the ground. All the trappings of life. Becker held the pillow down hard over his head hoping this regular, ordinary morning would go away; fantasizing it was a lover in the kitchen with his mother, pressing her up against the ironing board and taking her standing up, panties around her ankles. Becker started to masturbate with that thought in mind, but couldn't sustain it, couldn't keep the image from dissolving into ludicrous parody.

Several times before, on the occasion of a handicapped person's murder or a statue's decapitation, he had been tempted to confront his friend. To reveal to him that he knew who was responsible, that he should give himself up or seek some kind of psychiatric help. But Becker had always held back, knowing his friend would deny it, perhaps laugh in his face. After all, where was the proof? And he knew it would be almost impossible to catch his friend in the act. Still, he followed each case religiously from ardent beginning to listless conclusion. Invariably, they went unsolved and ended as abandoned files in the police department backrooms. "Motive," the detectives said. "Where's the motive?" Becker knew the motive but had no way of making the police understand. Instead, he had spent many hours in those backrooms, trying to decipher the pattern of the crimes so that he could be present to witness the next one, to catch his friend red-handed. There was no pattern that he could see. First, a hydrocephalic dwarf was suspended by the neck from the roof of a 13-storey building. Then, the pigeon-shit-encrusted breasts were blown off Joan of Arc, the biggest piece no larger than her nipple. Following that, an elderly woman suffering from elephantiasis was suffocated and her giant legs meticulously sliced and deveined. Always, a lengthy period elapsed between one act and the next, between the murder and the mutilation. Never before had the two crimes been committed so close together. He was becoming desperate and thus careless. Patience, Becker told himself. Patience. The thought of confronting him was exquisite. Becker squirmed in bed, no longer able to lie still. His name was called out from the kitchen, followed by the announcement that breakfast was on the table. He refrained from answering and instead raised the volume of the radio. What was suddenly making him so bold if not the knowledge, the secret knowledge? He leaned over and pulled the gun from the holster taped to the bottom of his bed. It was a snub-nosed .38, oiled and loaded. He'd picked it up a year before after seeing it dropped into a downtown garbage can. When he'd first handled it, the barrel was still warm – and one bullet was missing. He sat up, twirling it on his finger and pointing it out the window at Cronos, happily serving as a repository for birds.

"Come on, you fucking fake," he said, imitating his friend the anarchist. "Move a fucking millimetre and I'll blast you to fucking smithereens."

Becker's notebook II:

For several days, while my parents concentrated on the income taxes, I sat cross-legged and utterly motionless in the cellar, sharpening my willpower and blocking everything else out. When I finally did meet up with my childhood friend, I would have to be prepared for any sort of treachery. He might plead with me, for example, hoping I would lower my guard long enough to be disarmed. Would he then be able to kill someone who was neither cripple nor statue? Better yet, would he have the courage to do away with someone he knew, a childhood buddy? Why not? I was ready to do it for the greater good, why not he for his own very clear, if peculiar, motives?

One evening, as his parents worked their way down to the final calculations, the exempted exemptions and discredited credits, Becker left the house by the basement door and, portable short-wave radio in hand, took the bus downtown. Finding his friend would be no problem, as he had provided Becker with specific directions the one time he'd written: "Sit right beneath the front legs of the rearing horse. Then, by looking straight ahead, extend the line made by the sword of the gaunt rider. At the end of it will be my apartment. You can't miss it."

A small, irritating and obviously imbecilic child sat beneath the raised hooves. He looked up with idiot eyes at the horse's bronze belly, looked up and laughed. Then he started to climb awkwardly up its back. Becker glanced about for his mother. Several women – stooped, jowly legs spread and with their backs to him – were surgically removing chicory plants from the ground. The knives gleamed in their calloused, claw-like hands. There was no one else around. The child was having difficulty maintaining his balance. Becker walked by the horse twice before he acciden- tally lifted the child's leg (trying to keep him upright, of course) so that he screamed and fell over the other side. Becker whistled and moved along, turning around surprised when he heard the thud of the child's head striking the concrete base of the statue. The mother dropped her bags and waddled towards where he lay wail- ing. She picked him up, screaming in a language Becker had heard previously only on short-wave, then whacked him hard across the face and dragged him away. Becker sat down beneath the horse and followed the line of the sword. It pointed directly at a window above a seedy grocery store, the only window without curtains. He could see bright orange walls inside and could hear the faint sounds of free-form jazz. There was no music Becker detested more.

"The cripples, the mental deficients, the useless," his friend had written, "are destined to confront me. They're too dangerous to keep alive. Walking, crawling, slithering time bombs all of them – and without even knowing it. While they sleep the drugged sleep of innocence, sliding slowly into statuehood, I suffer for them. I will be damned for them."

In order to observe him more carefully, Becker stayed in the park as much as possible. There was a public toilet at one end where he could go to wash up and occasionally change his clothes, using the hot-air vents to dry them. For food, he relied on the straw-hatted, candy-stripe-suited hot dog man who pushed his little cart through the park twice a day.

As far as Becker could tell, his ex-friend never left the room. Occasionally at night, he peered out the window, always bare-chested and with his eyes blazing in the dark. Human to the unfailing end, passion had not left him. He stared directly at the statue, using an instrument that closely resembled a ship's sextant. It suddenly became very important for Becker to discover whether he was completely naked or only half-so. His life depended on his not having a stitch of clothing on. Becker slipped the gun from its holster and held it beneath his coat, barrel pointed in the direction of his friend's head. Many, especially lovers of statues, would have had Becker shoot him on the spot. I believe in justice, not revenge, he said. Besides, it would have been a miracle shot from that distance.

Becker's notebook III:

I should have known he'd have a woman with him: "When the time comes, I'll need a member of the opposite sex to soothe my conscience, to help me plan, to goad me on and to blame afterwards. She'll be fat and dumpy with folds of flesh hanging loosely over her abdomen. Her breasts will sag to her knees and flap about when she wiggles. Varicose veins will striate her legs. But beware of her face. It'll be that of an unwavering accomplice – soft-skinned, smooth and most of all angelic."

His description had been extremely accurate, as if he were talking about someone already well known. For the first two nights, the routine didn't vary. They kissed, lips mashing, tongue to tongue, in a thoroughly disgusting way, and then sank slowly to the floor, vanishing from view. It would have been simple for me to sneak closer and lodge a bullet in her thick back when they pirouetted and slipped away. But the time hadn't yet arrived. Then, arising on the dot half an hour later, she rested her breasts – her long pointed breasts – against the windowsill and lit a cigarette, blowing the smoke away in a careless manner.

"It'll be necessary that she do all the shopping for me. She'll throw on a dirty red blouse with stained armpits and will walk to the store below. We'll sit on the ledge chewing white bread and cucumbers. Despite her filthy appearance, she'll be a very dainty eater, careful to wipe every crumb from her face with the discarded blouse."

Right after the meal, he took out his sextant and a notebook. Wrinkling his brow, he made what seemed precise measurements of the statue, then inevitably became very excited after studying the figures in the notebook. The woman paid no attention to him. She stood against the far wall and massaged her breasts to the howl of a jazz saxophone from a tinny transistor radio. I almost wanted to rush up and offer them my radio – but thought better of it. Whenever he jumped up excitedly, she drew in her breath and the breasts popped straight into the air, exposing her rib cage. On the third night of my vigil, the light went out in his room. This was it. The calculations were finished and he was now ready for his latest crime wave.

Becker went to the nearby phone booth and dialled home: "Hello, hello. Is anyone there? He's leaving his room right now. Are you listening? Forget the goddam income tax – just this once. They're walking down the street arm in arm. As if they were lovers or something of the sort. Fancy him a lover! Yes, that's the problem with catching anarchists. Having no fixed principles, they can transform themselves into whatever is necessary to complete the task at hand. Look, to make matters even worse, they've stopped right in the middle of the street. Right in the middle! And they're kissing for all the world to see. Like real lovers. Listen!" Becker held the phone out so that whoever was on the other end could hear. It went dead.

It was later in the evening. The door to the apartment had been conveniently left open and Becker stumbled in, heading straight for the bed. Something green and slimy twisted the pit of his stomach. He had to lie down or suffer the consequences. The room smelled of unwashed clothes and rotten half-eaten cucumbers. Filthy underwear littered the floor. Things – creatures, microbes, whatever – crawled away to deeper hells. He tied a handkerchief across his mouth and fell back on the bed. His stomach settled, bringing with it a sudden rise in joy. He had witnessed a murder, a cruel and very brutal murder. There was the obvious urge to rush out and grab the first person who chanced by: "Look! Look! I've solved it. While all you good citizens shrugged your shoulders and feigned unconcern, I solved it. The Case of the Cripple Killer and Statue Decapitator has been blown wide open." It was a silly urge. Strangers weren't interested. They might take him for a madman or worse, ignore him, stepping by his body like they would the ragged lines of homeless sleeping with their heads on the curbstones. Instead, he called the police: "Hello. I want to report a murder. That's right. Just listen. Are you listening? Who am I? Never mind who I am. Their kisses became less and less frequent as they quickened their pace. Who? The anarchist and his accomplice, that's who. Out of the side streets… Where am I? Don't interrupt! Out of the side streets emerged scores of beggars, each asking for a dime, a nickel, some change, anything. It was dark. Many of the street lights had been sling-shotted and never repaired. Cripples in wheelchairs criss-crossed the sidewalks recklessly, taunting him, demanding preferential treatment. You can't do that with him. You can't—" Becker slammed down the receiver, waited a few moments and then called once more. "It's me again. Yes. I'm forcing you to listen. It might very well be a crank call but you can't take any chances, can you? The cripples didn't, couldn't know he was walking among them not out of pity but to choose a victim. Not as a Christ but as an executioner. I saw it, I tell you. She was a beautiful girl with long golden hair and blue eyes. She might have been a mermaid except that her left leg was missing from the hip. She stood among the other cripples like a queen, pulling on a filtered cigarette, occasionally adjusting her tank top to better expose her breasts. Why are you threatening me? He was the one who killed her. He followed her to the dark alley where she entertained her men for a price. Then, with his accomplice holding her down, he strangled her and cut out her tongue. That's right. Cut it right out. Just follow my directions and you'll find her."

Becker tied the handkerchief once again across his mouth and returned to the apartment. After his eyes accustomed themselves to the dark, the first thing he noticed was the sextant and, beneath it, the notebook. Numbers and crossed-out words covered its pages. There were several errors in the subtraction of one angle from another; also a division by zero and the square root of a negative number. In the closet, piled to the ceiling with musty, moth-eaten clothes, were several sticks of dynamite and detonation caps.

His instincts had been right all along. Neither returned that night. He waited with the gun beside him on the bed, determined to take both of them in. No resistance would be tolerated. And he knew one slip-up would mean the end of him. His friend had displayed his ruthlessness on many occasions – that night had been only one more example. At first, he tried to study more closely the figures in the notebook, trying to decipher what his friend would do next. But the odour from the clothes was intolerable. Not even the handkerchief kept it out. There was only one solution. He gathered them all and dumped them into the bath tub. A golden cockroach slithered from the faucet but he managed to crush it before it could escape. Then he went to the grocery store to buy Javel water and Spic And Span. The man behind the counter said "Hello" as if he knew him. Becker ignored the greeting, under the assumption there were plenty of people who resembled him. Nevertheless, he was glad to be back in the apartment. He poured the Javel over the clothes and scrubbed the floor till it sparkled in the moonlight. At midnight, he turned on the radio to listen to the High Mass.

The priest, chanting over the thunder of artillery fire and the occasional sniper bullet, had hardly got past the *Kyrie* when the service was interrupted by the bulletin Becker had been waiting for. The body of a one-legged girl had been found in a dark alley. But this time there was more – suspects, two former wheelchair athletes down on their luck. The motive was believed to be jealousy, jealousy of the fact she often entertained men in the alley. Plenty of witnesses were willing to testify against them, to say they had seen the ex-athletes mistreat the girl and often chase her from the corner. The two didn't improve matters by accusing each other of the crime. Becker rushed to the phone booth and dialled the police.

"You fools! You bloody stupid oafs! I know who killed that one-legged girl and I'll tell you right now it wasn't any jealous wheelchair guy. What am I talking about? The one-legged girl that was murdered tonight. Incompetent idiots!"

He hung up and felt the urge to stick his tongue out at them. Why should he give the police the satisfaction of capturing his friend? He had done all the important legwork in the case and deserved the reward – if only moral – for bringing him in. He dialled the house again. The phone rang on and on. He was about to hang up in disgust when a tired female voice answered.

"Your son is on the verge of capturing the most wanted anarchist in the city," he said as rapidly as possible. "Anarchist. The one who's been causing all the havoc. Don't interrupt! No, I'm not coming home. I want you to get the reward. Didn't you hear me? That's right. The reward. Aren't you going to thank me?"

She didn't thank him, but he knew she would later. The clothes smelled very clean; the floors sparkled. In Sydney, Australia, the High Mass was in full progress and the participants – mostly recently-converted aborigines – had just been invited to receive the body and blood of Christ Our Lord. To the accompaniment of dijiridos, Becker picked up the sextant and aimed it at the statue. He marked down the various angles between horse and rider and compared them to those already written on the paper. There was a slight difference between them. He noticed it was the same number as that circled on the top right-hand corner of the sheet. He marvelled at his friend's ingenuity. He had gone to the trouble of fixing the angles so that anyone checking them would become convinced by his argument that statues moved, even if imperceptibly. But he couldn't fool Becker. In fact, he was foolish to try. "You couldn't fool an old pro," Becker would say as he and his accomplice walked in. "No way."

After having slept all the following day, Becker awoke at sunset, positive of his friend's next crime. He undid the string about his neck – connected to the door so that the slightest movement would be relayed to him – and took up a position near the window. The park slowly emptied of chicory women and hot dog vendors until only one man remained sitting on a bench. He was totally immobile. For a moment, Becker didn't recognize him – but only for a moment. For wasn't that his caped accomplice making her way through the park, gliding like a stingray towards the statue? She stopped before it and pulled an object from a shopping bag. The man shielded her from Becker's view. Then, seconds later, they moved away again, cleverly heading in opposite directions.

Twenty minutes passed before the statue exploded. Dust rose into the air and a small piece of bronze burst through the window of the grocery store below where Becker stood. When the dust settled, he could see that neither the horse nor the rider had its head. There were sirens; police cars screeched onto the grass from all directions, surrounding the park. Officers with flashlights moved back and forth, examining the severed heads, nudging them with their feet and finally placing them in clear plastic bags. Becker felt a certain pride in having guessed right once again.

And now they would no doubt be returning. Aha! Speak of the devils. Two shadows moved close to the wall of the building and disappeared up the stairs. Becker scrambled back behind the door, gun at the ready.

Becker's notebook IV:

They came in together and made immediately for the window. Both were laughing hysterically. His hands had already slipped beneath her dirty red blouse. She squirmed in his grasp, reaching into his pants. Their faces, lit up by the police cars, glowed a blood red.

I let them play out their little game of joy. They would only suffer more for it later. Still laughing, they undressed each other. More dirty underwear fell to the ground. Neither of them removed their socks as they embraced and sank to the floor. I waited nervously for them to begin their copulation so that I could capture them right in the middle of it. But as soon as they fell behind the window, as soon as they were out of sight, they set to kicking and punching each other. She called him a vile name and tried to knee him in the crotch, forcing him to protect himself with his hands. He levelled a blow at her chest. I jumped from behind the door, gun trembling in my hand but the rest of me steady, steady as a rock.

"That's enough. That's quite enough."

Becker had wanted it to be a basso-voiced command, but it came out a falsetto plea.

"Stay exactly where you are. Don't move."

The girl shifted to cover her massive body. Becker could see now she wasn't more than a teenager.

He turned to his ex-friend.

"Recognize me?" Becker asked, aiming the gun right in his mass of pubic hair.

The ex-friend shook his head.

"How about now?" Becker said, leaning closer. He shook his head again. "Oh, I see. That's the little game you're gonna play. Well, that's fine. That's just fine. Maybe a quick trip to the police station will jog your memory."

"Police station?" his ex-friend said defiantly. "What for? We haven't done anything. This is a free country, you know."

"You might be able to fool others with that 'why me? what have I done?' look of innocence – but not me. Don't you dare try it on me."

The girl began to sob, her entire body heaving with the effort. Her breasts slapped up and down wetly; her flabby thighs flattened against the floor, leaving an outline of moisture. Becker liked her very much at that moment. Almost to the point of letting her go. Almost. He turned to his ex-friend again.

"Pretend I'm not here. Pretend I don't exist." His ex-friend didn't understand. For an anarchist, Becker could see he was a bit of a fool. "Come on. I'm going to sit back on the mattress now and put my feet on the windowsill. I want you to act as if you were alone, just the two of you, enjoying yourselves after another productive night of crime and general mayhem. First, turn on the light." The room regained its orange glow. "Very good. Now you. Yes, you. Come over here and massage your breasts in front of the mirror. That's right."

Becker was completely dissatisfied with the mechanical, uninspired way they did things and so had them do it again. And again, for a third time. They were like toys going through their rounds. His ex-friend picked up the sextant; she massaged her breasts to the beat of the *Agnus Dei*; he put down the sextant; she inhaled; he marked his findings in the notebook; she exhaled.

"Now, there is one last thing we'll do before I turn you in to the proper authorities. Call it a humanitarian gesture, if you like. But don't try to escape because the gun will be right here in my pocket and I won't hesitate to shoot. A citizen's arrest is entirely legal, as you well know. Besides, I don't think too many would have much sympathy for someone who kills helpless cripples, now would they?"

He told them to get dressed. Then he handed his ex-friend the stick of dynamite and timing device he'd found in the closet. The three of them made their way uptown on an almost totally empty bus. Becker sat one seat behind them with his gun trained on his ex-friend's back. The girl made several attempts to attract attention by crying but a jerk of the gun cut her short. They got off the bus and walked several blocks. Becker tried to lighten the situation by making small talk but the two of them were curiously quiet. Almost morose.

"Well, here we are. You recognize the neighbourhood? No? That's good; that's very good. Defiant to the end. I like that. Okay. Get busy. I think you're familiar with the routine."

But his ex-friend couldn't do it. His hands trembled; his knees buckled. With a sigh of disgust, Becker took the dynamite from him, wrapped it himself about the neck of Cronos and set the timer at 30 minutes. Then he hailed a cab for the trip back to their room. Neither of them looked at him, although he was anxious to get their attention and even made an attempt at a joke. It was the one about why anarchists can never call a meeting. Becker wasn't insulted by the fact they didn't laugh. I'm terrible at jokes, he told them. Always have been. He paid the cab and ushered them back into the room.

"You probably thought you'd never be caught, didn't you? Well, truthfully, you probably wouldn't have been if it weren't for me. I worked hard at discovering you and even harder at capturing you." They stood nervously against the bed, holding hands. Becker considered shooting them on the spot but that wasn't quite the ending he wanted, not this liquidy, oily finish. Then he had what he felt was a tremendous idea.

"Undress her! Undress her and make love to her. Quick! Right now! If you're really good I might even change my mind." They stared like two wax figures. "Come on!"

Becker's notebook V:

He wasn't very good. In fact, it was an utterly disgusting display. He sputtered and rolled on to her, struggling limply to penetrate. I sat on the windowsill and looked out, contemplating the useless vanity of human life. The girl tried to use her fingers to guide him but it didn't help. She closed her eyes. All the light vanished from her face. The last police car roared away in search of the vandal responsible for the wanton destruction of city property. I wrapped the gun in the girl's underwear and pressed the muzzle against his rocking back.

"Please," my ex-friend begged, coming to a standstill halfway from the ground. "I don't know you. I haven't done anything."

I ordered him to continue, promising not to kill him unless he stopped. I scanned their bodies, knowing the moment I came to their socks that I would go back on my word. He moved faster against her and there were even signs of genuine desire coming from them, the hint of a moan, the echo of a sigh.

Too late. The girl opened her eyes bright and wide at precisely the moment Becker squeezed the trigger. Her face was truly angelic, frozen by his bullet. The two bodies thudded together against the mattress and spasmed. Similar trickles of blood flowed from the corners of their mouths. It was then that Becker realized it had been his intention all along not to subject them to the processes of law and justice. It would have been immeasurably cruel for an anarchist and his accomplice and he was inexorable but not cruel.

He pulled the covers over them so that only their faces showed. There were four minutes left. He turned out the light but left the radio on. The Mass was being held in Los Angeles, gospel singing from East L.A. Once again he dialled home. This time a male voice answered. He tried to imagine it wasn't his stepfather, his bald tax accountant stepfather at that very moment working over the receipts, trying to squeeze more blood out of them, to induce deductions; he tried to imagine a lover maybe, a bull-fighter, a mountain climber, a porno-flick star – but he couldn't.

"Hello, pseudo-dad? The city is safe at last. No more anarchist menaces running loose. Who's this? Your son. Drunk? I'm not drunk. I never drink. You really know a lot about me, don't you? I bet you sleep with your socks on, too, don't you? Listen, Dad. I called to tell you that in…in two minutes… Listen! You know that statue in the backyard? The bird bath, idiot! Well, I left some-thing there for you and Mom. It's a surprise. A little something to help you pay those nasty tax bills. Hurry or you might miss the fun."

There was static in the air and particles that looked like soot floating down from the sky. Becker slammed down the phone. It was then he noticed that his hands, also covered with soot, needed cleaning. With a feeling of utmost satisfaction for a job well done, he pushed open the door of the underground public washroom and stepped in. Applause came from all the stalls and booths. There were statues leaning against the walls clapping their hands so quickly the human eye couldn't follow; there were others sharpening swords and putting on armour. He recognized Heph-aestus, ugly and lame, but with his golden assistants all about him. And Cronos, preparing once again to dethrone his father. Then the statue of a blond-haired girl with one leg hopped over and pushed herself against him.

"Congratulations," she said huskily, before a tongue fell out of her mouth and she could speak no more.

Becker smiled and his face cracked. Things were speeding up around him, whirling faster and faster in the dense light. Or he was slowing down. It made no difference. As the first strains of a final High Mass rang through the washroom and out into the world, he was already well on his way to composing an appropriate epitaph, the words with which to protect himself.

Becker's notebook VI:

From myself.

THE BOX

The three scientists – two males and one female, all dressed in traditional white lab coats – stood around an opaque coffin-like box, opened at the top. A laser beamed down on the box from the ceiling. Aside from a computer terminal, a printer and several chairs, there was nothing else to attract the eye. Unless you counted a red light across the top of the door that blinked on and off: Electronically Sealed. Authorized Personnel Only. Illegal Entry Punishable Under the Canadian Security of Information Act.

"I don't know how much longer we can keep this up," Dr. Levitt, the older male scientist, a distinguished-looking man with hair greying at the temples, said.

"We've tried everything, Dr. Levitt," Dr. Pedersen, the female, said. "Nothing so far has affected it in any way—"

"That we can measure," the younger male interrupted.

"Of course, Dr. Greshner," Levitt said impatiently. "That's understood. We can't very well measure what our instruments can't measure, now can we?"

"I'm not so sure of that," Pedersen said. She took off her thick glasses and rubbed her eyes. A not unpleasant-looking woman of 45 or so, if not for the worry lines across her brow.

"Just exactly what do you mean?" Levitt asked.

"Nothing really. Except that… I get the feeling sometimes we're going about this the wrong way."

"The wrong way? And what is the right way?"

"I don't know, Dr. Levitt. I don't know."

"I see," Levitt said – and resumed circling.

On closer examination, it became apparent that the object was acting in a way no normal box would. For one thing, it didn't rest on anything solid but seemed instead to float just above the ground – as if in a state of permanent levitation or at least repulsion from physical objects. For another, its interior was pulsing softly, giving off a light that could be seen barely spilling over the top edge. And there were black markings on its sides, like stylized wings.

"Any reaction?" Levitt asked, leaning over but making sure not to get too close.

"As unresponsive and as touchy as ever," Pedersen said. "Nothing we do changes its state. Call it a permanent alarm system."

"Hmmm. Dr. Greshner, do we have audio amplification?"

"We do," Greshner said. "But we keep it at the lowest possible setting. It's quite painful."

"Painful or not, I would like to hear it."

Greshner walked over to the computer terminal and tapped the keyboard. Immediately a sound that combined the wails of someone who's just lost a child with the screeches of a tortured parrot echoed in the room.

"Thank you," Levitt said, gritting his teeth. "That'll do. Dr. Pedersen, any opinion as to what it might be saying?"

Pedersen shrugged her shoulders: "Pain, loneliness, death rattle, joy, an attempt at communication. Of course, that's assuming it's alive and what we're hearing is its language. We may be dealing with strictly automatic reactions. Or, at the most, sequentially activated. Like a radioactive material giving off signals as its atoms break down. That would explain its unchanging nature."

"I appreciate the hard work you've both put in," Levitt said. "We're just like a family here. However, I think the point is rapidly approaching where we may need a fresh start. Our benefactors are becoming anxious."

"Understood," Pedersen said. "Just give us—"

Levitt's cellphone beeped.

"Duty calls," he said, pressing his hand against the wall and causing the door to slide open. "I expect a report the moment there's a breakthrough."

Before the door closed again, they caught a glimpse of him berating the janitor, pointing to a spot on the floor that obviously hadn't been cleaned to his satisfaction.

"I expect a report the moment there's a breakthrough," Greshner said in mock imitation. "Just like a family, indeed. Who the hell would want to be part of that old fart's family?"

"Easy there, Bill. The 'old fart' is rumoured not only to have a family but to have been mortally wounded by some who didn't quite measure up to his expectations."

"Nice guy. I bet he dropped them because they hadn't been nominated for Nobel Prizes before turning 30."

"Such bitterness – and I heard him say he considers you a replacement for the son that never panned out."

"Bullshit! I'd rather be disowned."

"Come on, Bill. There are worse things in life than working for Levitt Labs. In fact, it's quite a cushy job, isn't it? Why, can't you see yourself – white-haired, rheumy and loaded down with honours – reminiscing about the good old days with your favourite white rat?"

"Thanks a lot. Pretty soon you'll have me manhandling the young techs à la Dr. Quisted."

"Now, now," Pedersen said, sitting in a high swivel chair overlooking the box, "let's not be too harsh on dear old Eric. After all, where would we be without his latest variation to the solution of the inter-twirled peanut butter-jelly dilemma?"

"A classic. I couldn't believe it when I heard that he'd been working on it for ten years. What's he got on Levitt anyway? Fudged results from Chem 101?"

"The truth is Quisted was once quite promising. In the days when this was still Levitt-Quisted Labs." She straightened her glasses. "Enough. Time to get back to work."

"Wait a minute. You can't just leave me hanging. I want the gossip, all the gossip and nothing but the gossip. How else am I gonna make my way up the scientific ladder?"

"There's not much to tell. A classic story: Levitt was the better administrator; Quisted, believe it or not, had an enviable reputation in the lab." She paused. "And before you hear it from someone else – yes, we were lovers once."

"You and Twist Top?" She nodded. "Jesus, I'd heard the rumours but... So what happened?"

"What happened?" Pedersen turned to look at the box. "Let's just say Quisted and I were working under different assumptions and definitions. He wanted me as one more example of his conquest of approaching old age; I wanted him as the father I never knew. That obviously couldn't last."

"Wow, you and Quisted...who would've—"

"Okay. Back to work. Let's go over those printouts again."

"You know that we could do this more easily on a monitor," Greshner said.

"Yeah. Just call me old school."

"Okay," Greshner said, holding up the two-foot thick pile of computer printouts and then letting it drop to the cement floor. When the echo died, he sat cross-legged in front of the printouts and began to read: "Program One: Input consists of one smooth-surfaced box-like object made of unknown material. Dimensions: two metres long by one wide by half-a-metre deep. Weight: Unknown or none, depending on your outlook. Closed on all sides except for the top." He looked up at Pedersen who had joined him on the floor. "That is all the empirical data, at least all that makes any sense. As for the rest, pretty scant. 'Object brought in under closest military guard. Location Found: Queen Charlotte Islands. Origin: Unknown. Metallurgical, chemical, atomic analysis not performed due to inability to scrape sample material from box. Scanners opaque. Results nil. Characteristics: Floats 10 centimetres above rest position. No visible means of support or energy emission. Attempt to push it down displaces it easily but on release results in automatic return to equilibrium but without any intermediate phases that can be detected, either by eye or on film. Interior – which is completely transparent and seems empty – gives off a light pulse whose timing varies, no two being the same. Once again, no energy measurements obtained from pulse and no source for pulse. Exterior: Unidentified stylized markings that also pulse.' And there you have it. Except for the response reaction, that's it."

"You know, Bill," Pedersen said, "I'm getting a funny feeling about this. Like we're missing something obvious. Or being betrayed by our own instincts."

"My instincts tell me we should start over again and re-examine every bit of evidence we've collected in the last six weeks."

"Okay, Bill, as long as Levitt Labs is paying us, let's just do that, shall we?"

She lowered her head and started to work her way through the printouts. Greshner went over to the terminal and tapped away on the keyboard. The printer spewed out more of the paper. This continued on for several hours, during which neither spoke. Finally, Pedersen stretched and pushed the paper away from her.

"I've had it," she said. "Break time. I think I'm ready to face that hospital cafeteria."

Pedersen placed her palm against the wall. The door opened. The janitor, a hunchbacked man in his mid-30s, stood in the corridor with a wet mop in his hand.

"Hey, Red," Greshner exclaimed, holding out his hand for a high-five, "how are we this afternoon? Doc Levitt been hassling you again, huh?"

Red, obviously named for the shock of curly hair that shot up in all directions, smiled shyly. He tried to speak but it took him a few seconds before the first garbled words came out.

"Oh n...no. He's a n...nice m...m...man. He f...found me th...th...this job."

"Sure he is. But how goes it, huh? Win any dance contests lately?" Greshner turned to Pedersen. "This boy's quite a ballroom dancer, you know. Takes lessons at the 'Y'."

"Really?" she said. "You'll have to teach me sometime. I've always wanted to learn how to dance. Can you do that?"

"S...sure, D...Dr. Ped...Peder...sen. B...back hurts r...right now th...th...though." He looked at Greshner. "Maybe y...you could h...have a l...look, eh, d...doc?"

Red giggled, his blue eyes shining in appreciation of the joke.

"A real comedian, this boy," Greshner said. "And to think all that talent's going to waste. What a shame."

"My m...mother thought I w...was f...f...funny, too," Red said, turning to Pedersen.

"What are mothers for?" she said.

• • •

The cafeteria did indeed resemble a hospital's attempt to cheer up its patients. While the rest of the building's dominant colour scheme was white on beige (so that even three-dimensional objects seemed to fade away), the cafeteria was a sunburst of patterns with the walls a repetition of black and yellow checks, enlivened by green polka dots, and the plastic moulded chairs and tables a sickly mauve. Rumour had it Levitt commissioned the cafeteria on the cheap from an interior designer specializing in mental facility nurseries.

"And barf," Greshner had said the first time he'd seen it. "It's like they let a whole bunch of winos in and shoved fingers down their throats."

No sooner had they bought coffee and seated themselves than Dr. Quisted burst through the door, smiled brightly at a young female technician and then headed their way.

"Ah, Bill," Quisted's friendly voice boomed in greeting, as his hand came down on Greshner's shoulder, "trying to avoid me again, eh?" He nodded curtly towards Pedersen.

"Eric, we'd be more than glad to have you join us. But, as you can see, this is a two-seater and Levitt, in his wisdom, had the tables and chairs bolted to the floor so…"

"No problem, Bill. I just came over to congratulate you on the fine job you've done since joining the lab. And don't let Levitt's gruff façade fool you. He actually thinks highly of you."

"Well, most of the credit should go to Dr. Pedersen. It was her translation program that allowed us to get as far as we are today."

"Of course, of course. I didn't mean to imply—"

"No implication taken," Pedersen said, tilting sugar into her coffee before remembering she drank it black.

"At any rate, Bill, keep it up. I look forward to working with you in the future."

With that, he patted him on the back again, then turned and walked away.

"What the fuck did he mean by that?" Greshner said.

"Forget it, Bill. He's just trying to get even with me, that's all. He can't let it slide that Levitt picked me to head the project and not him."

• • •

Pedersen and Greshner worked on solving the box for the rest of the week, with Pedersen becoming progressively more morose and uncommunicative. Finally, she spent an entire morning just sitting in her chair and staring at the object, her head hanging just above the pulsing opening. Greshner had to call her name several times before she snapped out of it.

"Sorry, Bill. Daydreaming, I guess."

"You daydreaming! That's supposed to be my department."

"Actually, I was thinking of an entirely new approach. Like what if I take off my clothes and jump right in?"

"Anne, I think it's time for a nap," Greshner said, feeling her forehead. "Besides, you'd only bounce off. Like that pen a coupla weeks back."

The following evening at the weekly meeting of the lab's senior scientists, Quisted wasted no time in bringing up the subject of the strange object.

"I'm sure we all appreciate the effort put in by Anne," he said, all the while looking at Levitt. "I, for one, have had a long acquaintance with her work. But, in this case, the results have been underwhelming. Surely, it's time to try a new approach."

Everyone looked at Pedersen, waiting for her to explode as only she could when threatened professionally. But she just sat there scribbling, making circles on her memo pad and humming to herself.

"Have you a particular approach in mind, Eric, or are you just speaking generally?" Levitt asked when he saw there'd be no response from Pedersen.

"Well, I do happen to have one," Quisted said quietly. "What I'd like to try – or see tried at any rate – is something harder. More of a classical handling of the object with full scale use of the lab's facilities and personnel. Off the top of my head and rather crudely, I can think of electric shock, drugs, minor dissection perhaps. Obviously, some gamma ray bombardment and lasering to test its limits. I'm aware there are some who contend this thing is not only alive and sentient but conscious in a unique way and at least able to produce symbols. That, to me, is poppycock, pure and simple. As scientists, it's our duty to get back to the conducting of scientific experiments, to collecting that data and making sense of it."

Levitt turned to Pedersen who was still obliviously scribbling in her pad: "Anne, would you care to present a rebuttal?"

Pedersen kept her head down for a full five seconds, then looked up and said: "Eric is right. I have no objections to his taking over. Now, if you'll excuse me."

With that, she arose and walked out of the conference room, leaving behind a bewildered and murmuring group that couldn't figure out if they'd won or been totally routed. Instead of returning to work, Pedersen took off her lab coat and left the building. Outside, she was nearly blinded by the late-afternoon sunshine. She couldn't remember the last time she'd been out of Levitt Labs before dark.

• • •

Once in her condo apartment, the first thing she did was shut down her cellphone. Then she poured herself a stiff drink and, wrapped in a blanket, went to sit on the balcony to watch as the sun set in the west over the ever-crumbling, ever-renewed CN tower, wrapped in its construction shell. She looked out at a vast sprawling place that was well into its old age: sedate, steady, fat in the middle, a bit maudlin and sometimes forgetful that it had been created for the use of the people who lived in it. And yet also dangerous for the undercurrents, the pockets of resistance. It was as well strangely debilitated. It seemed that no matter how quickly they put up new buildings, they were devoured by rust, by leaks, by cracks. She'd heard cases where the bottoms of structures were actually crumbling before the tops were put on. Levitt Labs was the exception. But then no one lived there and it gave off a purely artificial warmth out in the pristine suburbs. Now, there was one more strangeness, one more unexplainable variable in the equation. She had almost managed to fall asleep when the doorbell rang. She leaped up, lost for a moment in the dark, then shivered and went inside. The bell rang again.

"Okay, okay. Hold your horses."

She pressed the buzzer to release the high-rise's front door, then waited for her guest to make his way up the elevator. She had a pretty good idea who it would be – for she had no friends or social life outside the lab – and wasn't startled when she threw open the door.

"Hiya, Bill," she said. "Fancy seeing you here."

"What the fuck's going on?" he said.

"I gave up on the project, that's all. Wanna drink?"

"What do you mean you gave up? It's not yours to give up, dammit. And just dumping it in the lap of that poor excuse for a medieval torture master, that's…that's…"

"All I've got is Scotch and rye. Sorry."

"Anne, this is insane. You owe me an explanation."

"Okay, okay. Here, sit down. I haven't been able to explain it to myself as yet but maybe trying to tell you will make things clearer."

They sat down. Pedersen poured herself another drink and downed it in one shot.

"Ugh!" she said. "I hate booze."

"We were this close to a breakthrough," Greshner said, holding two fingers about a centimetre apart. "I could taste it. The results were starting to mesh."

"That's a pile of bull and you know it."

"All right, Anne. All right. So, we weren't getting anywhere but I never took you for a quitter. You told me yourself never to give up. There's always another angle, another way of looking at something. And even if there isn't, you just start over again."

"So, I lied," she said, rising and walking over to the balcony door.

"I don't think being flippant about it helps much."

"Maybe that's what running out of lousy angles does to you."

"And two-bit philosophizing has never been your style either, Anne."

She shrugged and returned to her seat.

"Come back," Greshner said. "Tell that weasel Levitt you had a sudden lapse. You, of all people, are entitled to one. Tell him you'll take some of Twisted's suggestions under consideration. Tell him anything but don't leave me stranded like this."

"You know, Bill, I never noticed how young you are. I bet you're at least 20 years younger than me."

"I'm 28. What's that got to do with anything?"

"Nothing, really," she said. "You'd better go now."

"I'll go," he said, "but not until I get an answer. I want you to come back on this project. Or at least give me an explanation of why you won't."

"The answer is no – at least not for the moment. As for an explanation, how about because I don't feel like it? How about because I'm getting bad vibes? How about it's feminine intuition?"

"Jeez," Greshner said in mock horror. "I never thought the day would come when I'd hear such words out of the mouth of the hard-assed Dr. Pedersen, terror to all those who dare say the word 'qualitative'."

"Well, it's come. Now get out of here."

"Can I at least keep you up on what's happening? I'd feel a lot better if I knew you were taking an interest."

"Yeah, sure. I'd appreciate that. In the meantime, I've some light reading to catch up on."

• • •

It took less than a week for Greshner to get back to her.

"You'd better get down here," he said. "I think there's something here you might like to see."

"Bill, I agreed to be your listening post but coming down there wasn't part of the bargain. Besides, I've got more important things to do with my days."

"Oh really? Like what?"

"Well, let's see. Yesterday, I discovered a neat little zoo on the East Side. A mini-zoo really, with cloned mini-animals. And today I planned to go to the university library and bone up on my mythology. It's something I've neglected shamefully. Tomorrow? Tomorrow, there's an exhibit of gravity-free Japanese rock gardens. So…"

"Are you finished?"

"I guess so."

"Well, get down here on the double. It's important. No, strike that. It's not important – it's crucial."

• • •

The first person Pedersen saw when she arrived at the lab was a barely recognizable Quisted, haggard-looking and completely worn out. He smiled wanly and held out his hands almost in a gesture of surrender.

"Hello, Anne," he said, without any of his usual bravado. "Glad you could make it down."

"Dr. Quisted," she said, then turned to Greshner who had just come running up. "Well, Bill. What does our esteemed Dr. Quisted have for us? Gonna show me a little laser slice of the beastie? A milky solution where it hangs in and out of the crystal-liquid state? Oh right. The massive shock treatment was a success, but the patient died. Right? No. Well, then, it has to be the deprivation tanks. Let me see. He cut it off from all sensation and it starved for lack of affection."

"Anne," Greshner said, touching her arm as the three of them walked towards the lab, "you're being mighty dogmatic."

"I guess that's about what I deserve," Quisted said. "It's just that…it's just…" At this point, he seemed almost on the verge of tears but then pulled himself together. "I was drooling to get my hands on that experiment – I don't deny it. But…and you have to believe me…I was also concerned with the way we were treating it. Like it wasn't just another problem for the lab to solve. Like there was something there that went beyond that."

"And so," Pedersen said, "you decided to re-introduce the strict standards of the scientific method."

"Anne," Greshner said, "Dr. Quisted subjected it to all the tests you mentioned – and some that are not quite on the up-and-up list. And—"

"And nothing happened," she said.

"How did you know that?" Quisted asked. They were in front of the door to the lab.

"Call it predictive ability on prima facie evidence. Better known as being able to read the bags under people's eyes. But I didn't have to be hustled down here to learn that. So, unless you have something else to say, I'm off to visit the rock gardens."

"That's the least of it," Greshner said, looking at Quisted.

"You go ahead," the older man said, rubbing his eyes. "I still find it difficult to believe."

"Anne, when I entered the lab this morning I found someone inside."

"Inside the room?"

"Inside the box, Anne. Inside the box."

"Oh? Anyone we know?"

"Red."

"Red? You mean the janitor?"

"That's right. I have no idea how he got in there but he was lying face up, peaceful as you please, eyes closed and hands crossed over his chest."

"At first," Quisted said, "we assumed he was either dead or in some comatose state, because we couldn't wake him. Or even get close enough to wake him. And the info-laser indicated no heart beat or brain-wave emanation."

"Only the familiar three-beat light pulse we've been monitoring all along," Greshner said.

"We worked on him all morning," Quisted said. "About an hour ago, we decided to take a break. When we came back, he was gone."

"Gone?" She looked from one to the other.

"Vanished," Greshner said. "Nowhere to be found. We've had people turn the lab upside down. We even sent a security guard to his apartment. Nothing."

"Anything left behind?" Pedersen asked.

"Funny you should ask," Greshner said, taking a postcard from his pocket and handing it to Pedersen. "Found next to the box. Must have fallen out of Red's pocket."

The postcard featured a red-lipped tongue-hanging-out totem pole with the inscription: "Legacy Pole at Windy Bay."

"Can I hold on to this?" Pedersen asked.

"Sure," Quisted said. "Our tests on it show nothing out of the ordinary."

Greshner pressed his palm against the wall and they entered the lab. Taking a deep breath, Pedersen felt a familiar rush at the sight of the box.

"So," she said, as she walked towards it, "let's see if I can recap. Dr. Quisted tries everything short of a controlled nuclear device to pry some information from this thing. And fails utterly, miserably, completely. Along comes Red the janitor and he is able not only to break the security code for this room but to wangle a trip inside the box without so much as lifting his finger. Then he disappears, not necessarily from the face of the earth but at least from this corner of it."

"There's something unnatural going on here," Quisted said, looking at Pedersen. "At first, I was desperate for it to be your fault, some miscalculation you'd made, some simple oversight."

"You've been looking for that miscalculation ever since Dr. Levitt handed the project to me. Well, in a way, I've been hoping it was my mistake, too."

"What do you mean, Anne?" Greshner asked.

"Bill, from what you've told me, I gather Red was probably leaning over the box – like so – when…"

"Anne! Be careful!"

Both Greshner and Quisted rushed up when they saw what she was about to do. But it was too late. Her centre of gravity was already too far forward and she toppled over on to the box. However, she remained there less than a second before bouncing back to her original position.

"Damn!" she exclaimed. "I thought for sure I'd be accepted this time."

"Anne!" Greshner said, holding her arm for fear she might try it again. "What the hell do you think you're doing?"

Pedersen smiled and gently passed her hand over the force field that protected the box from invasion – or intrusion.

"Neither of you get it yet, do you?" she said. "That's because even the best among us are so caught up in our own little worlds, we can't imagine anything outside of them."

"Anne, are you seriously saying—?"

"That innocent little pulsing box trapped within its own anguish – or whatever – is here to announce the end of our world as we know it—"

"But that's sheer nonsense, Anne," Quisted said, turning his back as if no longer wishing to look at the object of his perplexity. "Total madness. I can accept the fact it's something we've never encountered before, perhaps a peculiar local twisting of certain of our laws, a singularity of the kind some of the more outlandish probability rules have even predicted. But to go from there to the end of the world is to give credence to the worst kind of rabble-rousing post-millennialist preaching."

"Ah, but I didn't say the end of the world. I said the end of our world as we know it. Our world defined as that construct we've put together through constant testing and reiteration of cause and effect."

"Anne," Greshner said quietly, "before you go on, there's one question I'd like to ask. How do we prove it? And, when we have proved it, how would we know that it would stay proved?"

"Well, we could line up all the humans in the world and have them take turns hurling themselves at the box. Or, we could start by asking ourselves what Red has that I don't."

"Off the top of my head," Greshner said, "I would say an obvious physical deformity, a bad stutter and an IQ between 80 and 100 points lower than yours."

"But then again, has it occurred to you it may not be proof we want?"

"My God," Quisted said. "I can't believe what I'm hearing. This smacks more and more of a religious initiation. Next, we'll be bearing witness and setting up of a shrine to the gods of chance."

"Not the gods of chance, Eric. The gods of fate, perhaps. And hope."

"Hope, chance, fate – gobbledygook that has no place in our world. Not if we're to live by the hard and fast rules it's taken centuries and countless lives to develop. Are you saying we're to give all this up because some box doesn't seem to operate by the same rules? That's insane. Next, you'll be telling us we should go back to killing our first-born and burning witches."

Pedersen shrugged her shoulders: "What about you, Bill?"

"I'm confused, Anne. For one thing, I don't know the implications of what you're saying. For another, I can't imagine any other world but this one."

"Well, that's honest anyway."

She turned and headed for the door. Greshner joined her, leaving Quisted to stare at the box.

"What now, Anne?"

"Now? I'd like to get down to the library. There's some reading I have to catch up on. Why don't you come around at about eight? I might have something for you."

•   •   •

At the Robarts Library, Anne took down some books on mythology and sat at an empty desk. She started reading, but then drifted off into thoughts of what she'd be doing from that day forward, convinced her time at Levitt Labs was over. She spent several hours this way, alternating between the reading material and watching the plasterers and bricklayers who dangled from flimsy scaffolds to repair the library's ever-crumbling façade. One more building being eaten away. They call it acid-rain climate change ozone depletion, she mumbled. More like the decay of logical constructs.

"The key to this whole thing," she said to Greshner later that evening, "is Red. I'm certain of it. And I've got to find him."

"You mean *we've* got to find him, don't you?"

"No. Just because I'm through doesn't mean you are. You've got a great future at Levitt Labs."

"Anne, you must be joking. I've handed in my resignation."

"You silly boy, you," she said, touching his face. "But I'd be lying if I said I wasn't glad."

"Good. That makes two of us."

"But none of it will do us any good unless we can track Red down. Damn! He couldn't have just disappeared into thin air."

"Why not, Anne? If this box is what you've been hinting at, then anything's possible."

"There still have to be reasons for things. It might not be what we're used to but a teleology, a purpose, has to be there. Look, if we discount the idea of a coincidence between Red's lying down in the box and his disappearance, then we have to assume the box has something to do with the disappearance. Right?"

"Of course," Greshner said. "Red is where the box has sent him."

"Shit!" Pedersen said. "Where are those printouts?" She searched around until she pulled out the pile of printouts and scattered them on the living-room floor.

"What are you looking for?" Greshner asked.

"This," she said, handing him one of the sheets.

"This? It's just a description of the box. We've been over it dozens of times."

"That's right. And missed it each time."

"Missed what?"

"Remember I said something obvious? Read what it says under Location Found."

"It says: 'Queen Charlotte Islands.' So?"

"So! Tell me, what's on the Queen Charlotte Islands?"

"Anne, all I know is that they're on the west coast of British Columbia, near Alaska."

"That they are," Pedersen said. "And they just happen to be the ancestral home of the Haida people. In fact, they're now officially called Haida Gwaii."

"Okay, but what—"

"Recognize this?" Pedersen asked, opening up a book on Native American mythology.

"What am I looking for?" Greshner said. "I see a bunch of log cabins, totem poles, boats and what looks like furniture."

"The design on that bentwood box," Pedersen said. "Look familiar?"

"Holy fuck! That's the same design as on our box."

"Yep," Pedersen said. "And I bet you that's where Red is."

"Okay, Anne. But even assuming we're on the right track, those islands must cover a lot of territory. How exactly are we going to find Red?"

"This is where we're going to find him," Pedersen said, taking out the postcard.

• • •

It was easier said than done. When they landed at Sandspit Airport on Moresby Island and asked about getting to Windy Bay, they were informed that only tour boats went to Gwaii Haanas National Park Reserve – unless they were willing to kayak in the open sea. And, because it was considered sacred land, only a limited number of tourists were allowed in daily.

"But we're not interested in a tour," Pedersen said to the person behind the information counter. "We're going there to meet someone." She pulled out the postcard. "We shouldn't be there for more than a few hours at the most."

"Well, you can always charter a float plane," the information officer said and handed them a brochure with a list of float plane operators. "And, if you're not planning on going inland, you can skip the orientation course."

•   •   •

The view from the float plane was...other-worldly. On one side, the endless grey-blue of the Pacific Ocean; on the other, hundreds of dark-green islands in an archipelago of thundering water, dark looming temperate rainforests, and fog-misted mountain tops.

"I can see why the Haida want to preserve this," Pedersen said. "It's what Eden probably looked like."

"Yeah, Eden with vicious storms, bear warnings, and the occasional cannibal."

"Hey, nothing's perfect."

"What if he isn't here?" Greshner said.

"We'll enjoy the sights and leave. No harm done."

The plane landed in front of a barren, rock-encrusted landscape. As Pedersen and Greshner were taken ashore by boat, they could see the eelgrass and kelp forest ferns waving in the water beneath them. And, ahead of them, looming more than 40 feet into the sky, the Gwaii Haanas Legacy totem pole.

"We'll come back for you in four hours," the guide on the boat said after depositing them on land. "Please be ready to leave."

•   •   •

It was dusk and they had been standing in front of the pole for several hours when a figure emerged from behind it and walked towards them. In the dim light, it appeared as if the figure was shimmering or changing shape with each step it took. As if it had arms and legs one moment and wings, feathers and claws the next. But as it came nearer there was no doubt it was Red, although a Red who no longer stooped over.

"Greetings, friends," Red said with a smile and without a stutter. "Welcome to Hlk'yah GawGa. Or Windy Bay, as the colonizers might call it."

"Is that really you?" Greshner asked.

"As you can see, I'm a new man," he said.

"But…how…?"

"Dr. Pedersen. Naturally you must have a lot of questions. But before we get to them, you should know that you have been chosen for a special mission."

"A special mission?" Pedersen said. "Why me?"

"I don't know," Red said. "I suppose it's because your mind is more open than your colleagues."

"More open to what?" Pedersen asked.

"To what I am about to offer." Both Greshner and Pedersen stared at him without saying a word. "The promise of a new world."

"I don't understand," Greshner said. "Who can make such promises?"

Red took a crystal sphere about the size of a baseball out of his pocket and held it out for Pedersen.

"Take it, Anne. Don't be afraid. With it, you can bring light to the universe. With it, you'll release humans from necessity, from the weight of laws, from decay, from death itself."

Pedersen took the ball. It pulsed slightly and tingled but it wasn't an unpleasant sensation.

"What am I supposed to do with it?"

"Bring it back to its proper home."

"The box, right?" Greshner said.

"Exactly. All you have to do is roll the sphere into what you call the box. The rest will take care of itself. And don't worry about getting it through airport security – the ball will not be visible when it's not in Dr. Pedersen's hand. Any questions?"

"Yes," Greshner said as Pedersen shook her head and continued staring at the ball. "You've explained why Dr. Pedersen, but why you?"

"Why me? I don't know. I do know that I will be responsible for ushering in this new world. That my powers will include the ability to shape things – in a way that you would consider magical and thus impossible. I will be me – and not me. I will be a hemlock needle, an infant, a sharp-beaked bird. I will be here and I will be everywhere."

"What…what will this new world look like?" Pedersen asked.

"Look around," Red said. "Here everything has a purpose. Even decay."

"One last question," Greshner said. "Why don't you finish the job yourself? Why bring us in at all?"

"Because the moment I took my place in the box," Red said as he slowly walked away, starting to shimmer and change shape once more, "I could no longer perform the tasks of this world. Only you can do that."

"And what happens," Greshner shouted at the receding figure, "if we can't deliver the sphere, if we have an accident or something along the way?"

"Or if I refuse to place the orb in the box?"

"Sadly, the box and orb would vanish again for another millennium."

He waved to them, arms and wings mixed up in the motion. Then he turned and disappeared behind the totem pole.

• • •

When they arrived at Pedersen's the next evening, Levitt and Quisted were waiting.

"Excuse me," Pedersen said, "I must have the wrong apartment."

"This is no time for jokes," Levitt said. "Where have you been?"

"Where we've been is none of your business," she said.

"May I remind you –"

"No! May I remind you –"

"Please, Dr. Levitt, Dr. Pedersen," Quisted said, holding out his hands. "This is getting us nowhere. Anne, we apologize for the intrusion. The superintendent let us in when we told him who we were and that it was an urgent matter."

"I see," she said. "And, pray tell, what matter of urgency may it be?"

"It's that damn box," Levitt blurted out. "It won't stop howling. We can't turn the noise off. Or at least the incompetents" – he looked at Quisted – "I employ at the lab can't."

"Okay," Pedersen said. "So, what do you want from me?"

"I thought perhaps," Levitt said, "as you set up the translation program you might know a way to turn it off. Or, at least to make it bearable."

"I might," she said. "But right now, I need my beauty rest. I'll come down to the lab first thing in the morning."

• • •

The next morning Pedersen and Greshner were silent on the drive to the lab. They drove through some of the city's worst slums, mostly empty shells slated for demolition, rusted tin shacks resembling the favelas of Brazil. Ahead of them, on the edge of the

115

destruction, like a squat white larval beast devouring the country-side, Levitt Labs waited. The security guard at the front gate waved them through. Levitt and Quisted stood at the lab door, not wanting to go in one minute too soon.

The moment the door opened, a blast of sound hit them, a high-pitched screech-cum-moan-cum-signal for help.

"We've shut down the laser, disabled all input and output to it," Levitt shouted, hands clasped tightly over his ears.

Pedersen approached the box. She stopped beside it, beside the chair she'd occupied for six weeks. As she stood there, the howling seemed to increase in strength, become more insistent. It was as if the box knew it was being isolated and she had something it wanted, something it needed badly to reverse the process. Pedersen looked into it, into the unceasing, unchanging pulse. She pulled her hand out of her pocket, holding the orb. It glowed and pulsed at the same rate as the box.

The others fell back as if they had been violently pushed away. Pedersen held the orb above the box. A beam erupted from the box and enveloped the orb. She felt the warmth surround her. She saw fields that resembled Elysium, super-human creatures without a care in the world, lush forests sending out signals to the rest of the universe – and, at the centre of it all, Red in all his glory, black-plumed, fierce-eyed, grinning. "Oh my," she said, as she lowered her hand towards the box, held the orb upside down, prepared to release it.

And then threw it against the back wall before collapsing to her knees.

The box moaned once – and vanished. The orb bounced before it too disappeared.

"What the hell just happened?" Levitt demanded after recovering his senses. "You were supposed to stop the howling. Not make it disappear."

"Thank you," Greshner said, helping her up.

"What are you thanking her for?" Levitt said. "We had a contract to fulfill. That box was supposed to be handed over to our benefactors."

"Benefactors?" Greshner said. "You mean the war mongers."

"Don't be so naïve," Levitt said. "They pay our bills. We wouldn't survive without them."

"Sorry," Pedersen said, still trying to catch her breath. "But I'm not sure you'd like the alternative."

"This is sabotage," Levitt said.

"That might be a little difficult to prove," Greshner said.

"What! I've got you as witnesses," Levitt said. "And all the computer data."

"I didn't witness a thing," Quisted said.

"Nor I," Greshner said.

"And that so-called computer data is completely useless," Pedersen said.

"This is outrageous," Levitt said, stalking out of the lab. "You're all fired. Scientists like you are a dime a dozen."

"Perfect timing," Pedersen said. "The three of us are thinking of starting our own lab."

"We are?" Greshner said, startled.

"Nothing extravagant, mind you. Just a place to investigate some of the basic phenomena. Have you ever noticed how the basic phenomena get ignored, Dr. Quisted?"

"Yes," Quisted said, "a little too much emphasis on mixing peanut butter and jelly."

"Get out!" Levitt yelled.

As the three walked towards the exit, Red, once more stooped and shuffling, came around the corner pushing a bucket with a mop in it.

"Red," Pedersen said. "I'm so sorry."

"Maybe next time," he whispered as he shuffled by, mop slapping against the floor.

"What?" Pedersen said. "What did you say?"

STRANGERS

"I'm tired of knowing you so well," I say, lying in bed beside you propped on a pillow. "I'm tired of your pleasant smile and your boundless patience; your never-say-die attitude and your unflagging energy. Why is it my food's never burnt? Not even slightly overcooked. And what's the reason for having the bathwater always so absolutely perfect? Perfect temperature; perfect level; perfect round bubbly suds? In short, I'm tired of having you know me so well, so intimately, and yet without words. Do you hear me?"

You, of course, pretend not to, pretend to be asleep, your back turned to me, warm flesh – where exposed – rising and falling calmly, predictably, mouth slightly open and the breath exhaling softly through your nostrils. You turn languidly towards me. Look at that, will you? Not a crust on your eyes; not a speck of dried foam on your lips; not a hint of sour breath. Nothing to indicate, mere moments after you awake, that you've been sleeping, that your stomach has been digesting bits of acid-coated food, that your bowels are bursting with gas.

"I've heard it said, through reliable sources, that others nag their lovers constantly, forbid them certain necessary privileges, demand money, make them feel guilty for the slightest indiscretion, the teeniest deviation from the straight and narrow. That's what I've heard said. And from unimpeachable sources. You! You forgive and forget. You satisfy my every need, no matter how outlandish. And, when you find yourself unable to do so, you give me money to go satisfy myself as I see fit. Bah, you disgust me!"

I lift my arm as if to strike you across the face, across the delicate alabaster face, upturned in its saintly posture of repose. The arm trembles above you (as it has done countless times before), quivering with a rage of its own, but then falls back (as it has done countless times before), tamed and useless. I was once told, prior to your knowing me so well, that a fierce animal in a zoo – a tiger, I think, or a leopard – escaped from its cage and ran for miles through streets filled with juicy humans simply to lie at your feet, to allow itself to be petted by you. Is it true? You shrug.

"Darling, let's play a game," I whisper close to your ear, your delicate ear, holding back an urge to bite it off. "That's it! An exciting, invigorating game. Some way to get to unknow each other again. Just like the old days. We'll drive to a field outside the city, to a—"

Shivering, you suddenly sit bolt upright on the bed, like a spring folded in half perhaps or a trap set to catch some invisible prey, your eyes wide open yet, for a moment, unseeing. You gasp, then blink and shake yourself awake. You throw the covers back and give me a kiss on the lips. Your mouth smells of flowers. Or is it ambrosia? I want to kiss you again, to pin you down and slide my hand down the front of your pink slip. But you roll over me playfully (oh my God! The scent of your body!) and walk away swaying, a long purple robe wrapping itself about your shoulders. I follow you and stand with my mouth to the washroom door, against the cold keyhole.

"About that game," I say, knowing persistence is the only thing that pays off. "It's one you like. We'll drive to a field on the outskirts of the city. You'll enjoy the country and the fresh air. Yes, you will. Once there, you stand at one end and I stand at the other. It doesn't matter which end. Oh, all right. You can have the side with the sun to your back. Is that okay?"

The toilet flushes, followed by the odour of lavender.

"Good. Here's what we'll do then. On three…let me think now. On three, we'll shout our names. No, in order to forget, we'll shout someone else's names. That's it. We'll shout the names of complete strangers and run towards each other. Not too fast and not too slow. What do they call it? Loping, that's it. Like werewolves do. Or tigers. Easy, eh? Very easy. We'll run through fields of red and orange flowers, pink and yellow flowers, tangerine and pale gold flowers – and embrace in the middle. A meeting to dispel one another, to repel the familiarity, to unspell our names."

The door flies open. You peck me on the cheek and brush past into the kitchen, combing your hair. Of course, it doesn't need combing. Nor does a single strand catch in the comb's teeth.

"I know, I know," I say, sitting in the chair across from you so that our knees touch (it's a small kitchen, a minuscule kitchen more like a broom closet than a kitchen). "We've played this game before. Four, no, five times. Well, anyway, many times. And you're fast tiring of it. But that's no reason not to play it once more, is it? Is it?"

The piledriver starts up outside the kitchen window. It is visible there, rising up and inserting thick steel girders into the ground, building up a small fortress of thick steel girders. Even with the window shut, that makes it very hard to converse. But I'm determined and start to shout above the din, above the shaking thunder of glass.

"Today would be a fine day on which to play the game. A fine day, I said. Do you hear me? A chance to escape all this, even if only for a couple of hours. What say you?"

You are holding a grapefruit in your hand which you cut expertly. It is my grapefruit. First, you make a general incision around the edge, disconnecting the rind from the meat. Then you sever the pieces, two by two, so they float in the fruit's own juices.

Finally, lifting it, you sprinkle sugar above and beneath it, rivulets of dissolving sweetness.

"It'll be such great fun," I say, opening my mouth and allowing you to spoon several pieces into it. "I know you'll enjoy it just as much as I do. And besides, it's not too often we get to do this. Especially on a summer day."

I'm finished eating. After wiping my mouth, you leave me to get dressed. I take the opportunity to examine the beautiful stiletto I carry Sicilian-style, tied to a string about my neck. It had been won years before at a church bazaar, the one prize I desired above all else. When we still made love, before the fear of disease drove all loving out of us, sometimes it dangled against your back (naughty, naughty), raking up and down your spine; other times, it hovered over what you called the "hot private parts" nipping and stinging like a puppy. It is, of course, my destiny to kill you with it, I whisper. In no time, you're out of the bedroom again.

"How come you dress so fast? Others I know take hours. Some even start the day before on really important occasions – and go all night without sleeping for fear of wrinkles. But you, you walk in nude and walk out clothed. Surprise me one day with your foolishness. Delight me with an ounce of high stubbornness, a stamping of delicate feet. Tell me I know less about you than I think. Tell me about your dreams before I created you."

You wear nothing but a sackcloth blouse and your favourite rubber boots. The ones scarred with makeshift patches. Your hair, now frizzy and unkempt, is tied back with a piece of black electrical wire. Purple lipstick is smeared across one side of your face, from earlobe to edge of mouth.

"You insist on making me admire you for your lack of taste. I must refuse, deny. And yet you take the refusal, the denial for a compliment. How is that possible?"

You hold my arm like a true lover and we step outside. The car – how red and sporty it looks – is still there, parked inches from the piledriver. I roll back the convertible top and we get in. It is thus we drive out of the city in search of the right field, a just-so field surrounded by large straight fir trees and perhaps resplendent with strawberry plants. Although the strawberries aren't necessary. Not really.

"I hope you're ready for this game," I say, patting you on the knee. "Mentally prepared, as it were. But, of course, you are. How many times have we played it now? Five? Yes, it must be five. It becomes easier all the time, doesn't it? No more worries about missing a step or going in the wrong direction or running by each other. And I know you enjoy it. Oh, there's no use denying the fact. It's written all over your face in bold letters. Here, let me read it for you: `I really enjoy the game. It's the kind of thing I could do forever. There's no better way to get to unknow each other.' See, I told you I could read faces."

We drive and drive. Over hill and dale. Over dale and hill. Nothing quite fits our needs. Those fields with flowers, even more colourful than expected or demanded, are already occupied by cows, intensely stupid cows, chewing, chewing. Or horses show-ing off their penises. Other fields, just a bit on the short side or without trees surrounding them, might have been suitable on pre-vious occasions or for future use. But not today.

"You understand, don't you, my dearest? Today of all days I want something ideal. What my mind's eye sees. I want the dream. Not a dream. *The* dream. You have dreams, don't you? Come on, don't deny it now. That's why you wake up so startled in the morn-ing, isn't it, with your eyes shut tight? You'd like to hold on to it, isn't that so? Hold on for as long as possible. That's why I always wake before you do. To catch you dreaming. But it doesn't help. Not in the least."

The car sputters, then runs out of gas and coasts to level ground. I try to coax it further but it's no use. This is it. The location has been chosen for us. All around us are fields choked with potato plants. No flowers, no trees. Not a hint of strawberries. Just row on row of young potato plants covered in pesticidal spray – and bright-coloured potato bugs writhing in their death throes. I open the car's glove compartment and pull out a gun, a cute little six-shooter peashooter which I hand to you. Then we climb the fence (watch out for splinters) and walk to opposite ends of the field. The sun shines directly in my eyes. I'm near tears.

"I'm sorry," I mumble, knowing you can't hear me. "I'm truly sorry our game must be played in such deplorable surroundings, amid potato plants. I would have hoped for more. But, never mind. It's the spirit that counts. Isn't that right? I'm sure it is. Are you ready?"

I reach into my shirt and unhook the stiletto, hefting it like an expert, an old pro. You adjust your boots and shake yourself from top to bottom.

"One, two, three."

I shout your name, your familiar name. You shout mine. Too late to remember we should have used pseudonyms. Real names can be dangerous. We start to run at one another. I trip on the first step and fall with my face in the dirt, sending up a puff of pesticide. But I am quickly up again, spitting sand. You dance towards me, all sweetness and light, the sackcloth heaving up and down, revealing your "hot private parts," a perfect patch of red hair like a triangular target. It's marred in the middle. Why did you have to mar it in the middle? Your face sparkles with a huge, beautiful grin, a fantastic, sensuous smile. I snarl and look grim. We draw closer together. Crows gather to gossip on the wooden fence posts: chattering chattering. They're talking about us, you know? Yes, they are. Potato plants fly into the air; potato bugs expire underfoot. We draw closer, smiling, snarling, laughing, grunting.

"Yes, we know each other too well. Too well. Your left nipple is smaller than your right. Just a touch smaller, mind you, but noticeable when aroused. You tell everyone who stares at you that your perfect teeth are false. That's a lie. You've carried my child within you for too long now and it's afraid to be born. Afraid it already knows more than it'll ever need to cope. That's another lie."

Steadily, steadily, only a few feet apart, the tiger and the leopard gone, your smile a radiant invitation to heaven, your feet floating slightly above the ridge-encrusted earth. Steadily, steadily, I unsheathe the stiletto, my stiletto, the one you've studiously ignored all these years, and plunge it sideways into your neck. Then pull it out again. Waiting for you to crumble. But there's no crumbling; there's no blood; there's only the tiniest pink mark on your neck. I fall back weeping, kneeling, jabbing the earth. You stand above me, feet apart, the sun blinding me, obscuring your face.

"The knife will always be the same," I blubber, "retracting when it touches your skin, folding within itself. Only a bazaar-won knife, you understand, useful for Cowboys and Indians and little kids who want to live again to die another day."

You push the gun hard against my forehead, between the creases of my forehead, cold against my flesh – and smile at me with perfect teeth.

"Five clicks," I say.

You nod. The farmer rushes down the hill, shouting. The crows burst into the air. My knife plunges in and out of the earth, leaving no dent. The gun – the gun – the gun—

Clicks.

The following stories, some in revised form, have been previously published in journals:

Exorcism: *West Coast Review* (1971)
Bandages: *Global Tapestry* (1988)
The Photographer in Search of Death: *Canadian Fiction Magazine* (1986)
Asgard's Light: *The University of Windsor Review* (1992)
Start: Nexus (1990)
Strangers: *Dandelion* (1987)
The Saviour: *Yak Magazine* (1988)
The Anarchists: *Truth Magazine* (2005)